The Little One

Lynda La Plante

**SIMON &
SCHUSTER**

London · New York · Sydney · Toronto · New Delhi

A CBS COMPANY

First published in Great Britain by Simon & Schuster UK Ltd, 2012
A CBS COMPANY

3 5 7 9 10 8 6 4 2

Simon & Schuster UK Ltd
1st floor
222 Gray's Inn Road
London WC1X 8HB

www.simonandschuster.co.uk

Simon & Schuster Australia, Sydney
Simon & Schuster India, New Delhi

A CIP catalogue record for this book
is available from the British Library

ISBN: 978-0-85720-920-7

Typeset by M Rules
Printed and bound by CPI Group (UK) Ltd, Croydon, CR0 4YY

MIX
Paper from
responsible sources
FSC® C014728

The Little One

... in Liverpool. She ... worked in ... eatre ... ion actress. She then ... and made ... breakthrough with the hit TV series *Widows*.

Her novels have all been bestsellers worldwide. Her script for *Prime Suspect* won many awards, and *Above Suspicion*, *The Red Dahlia* and *Deadly Intent* have been hugely successful for ITV in recent years.

Lynda La Plante was awarded a CBE in the Queen's Birthday Honours List in 2008. Her latest novel, *Blood Line*, went straight to number one.

Visit Lynda at her website:
www.laplanteproductions.com

Also by Lynda La Plante

Blood Line
Blind Fury
Silent Scream
Deadly Intent
Clean Cut
The Red Dahlia
Above Suspicion
The Legacy
The Talisman
Bella Mafia
Entwined
Cold Shoulder
Cold Blood
Cold Heart
Sleeping Cruelty
Royal Flush

Prime Suspect
Seekers
She's Out
The Governor
The Governor II
Trial and Retribution
Trial and Retribution II
Trial and Retribution III
Trial and Retribution IV
Trial and Retribution V

I dedicate **The Little One** to
Sara, Louis and Jacob

Chapter One

Barbara Hardy stared out of her office window at the heavy grey sky. It had been raining all day and London looked dreary and depressing. Without any warning, her heart suddenly started to beat wildly and she found it hard to catch her breath. Before she knew it, she was in the middle of a full-blown panic attack.

She tried to breathe deeply, she tried to empty her mind, but it was impossible. Instead she burst into tears. Too many things were going wrong in her life at the moment.

Her relationship with Gareth had just broken up. Even thinking about the rat made her gasp for breath again. Barbara had really believed that this relationship might last longer than her usual six months. And for almost a year things had been good between them. Then in the wine bar last night he told her that he'd met someone else.

Not only was she losing Gareth, but that morning she'd also been cornered by her landlady. If Barbara didn't pay the three months' rent she owed, she would have to leave her room.

And now she had to worry about her job. As a freelance, it was tough getting work these days. At present she was employed by a women's magazine and the editor, Mike Phillips, wanted to see her. Apparently her most recent piece had created some legal problems. She hadn't checked out the facts about a rock star's pregnancy and the magazine was in trouble.

Barbara was worried that this might affect her latest project. She had come up with an idea that she hoped would make her a great deal of money. She wanted to track down former soap opera stars for a 'Where Are They Now?' series. Mike had seemed keen when she first mentioned it and she had already approached a photographer friend called Kevin Shorter. He was to take shots of the actresses looking less than their glamorous best.

Barbara was not exactly looking glamorous herself when she went into Mike's office. It was hard to look good when she kept bursting into tears. Her eyes were red-rimmed and her nose was running as if she had a cold. What's more, her roots needed retouching.

Barbara had chestnut hair cut in a short bob, with auburn highlights. She was actually rather pretty, with a heart-shaped face, big blue eyes and a snub nose. Only her tight-lipped mouth took the edge off things. At thirty-eight years old she was still very skinny. She usually wore good casual clothes – short skirts, black tights and boots. Today she had chosen a tweed suit for her meeting with the editor.

Despite all her efforts, Mike barely looked at her. He simply told her that she was fired. What's more, because of the legal problems she had caused, the magazine would not be paying her the amount she had expected. Barbara was told to leave the building immediately.

As she made her way through the rain to the tube station, Barbara called Kevin, her photographer friend. She had intended to tell him that her idea for the series would have to be postponed. Instead, she found herself pouring out all her other problems.

It took a while for the awful truth to hit her and then she flushed with shame. She was not talking to Kevin at all, but to his partner, Alan. Alan was an actor and he hardly knew Barbara. However, he was a kind man and he told her that she could stay at their place. There was room just now because Kevin was away on an assignment.

Barbara could not believe her luck. Here was a chance to live rent-free, probably with decent food thrown in. Both men were very good cooks, while she could only just scramble an egg. She had no boyfriend, no job and only £250 in the bank. What's more, she had no family or close friends to turn to. As far as she could see, other people had such easy lives. It was about time something went right for her.

She thanked Alan and hurried back to her rented room. Ignoring another demand from her landlady, she packed up her belongings and left.

Alan and Kevin shared a small but lovely terraced house in Kingston, close to Richmond Park in south-west London. Alan showed Barbara to the spare bedroom. It was more like a box room really, a place for Kevin to store his equipment. Barbara was tearful as she told Alan how grateful she was. He smiled and said that she was welcome to stay until she found a new place to live.

Alan was a very good-looking man in his late thirties. He was blond and tanned, and he obviously worked out. He spoke in a deep baritone and did a lot of voice-overs for adverts on TV.

Once she had packed away her clothes, Barbara joined Alan in the kitchen. She burst into tears all over again as she explained how hurt she'd been by Gareth and then by losing her home. She didn't mention being fired. When Alan asked about the 'Where Are They Now?' series, Barbara found herself getting a bit carried away. She told him that it was a big commission for *OK* magazine, and the more she talked the more she began to believe her own story.

Alan offered her a cup of tea, then showed her around. He told her to make herself at home and gave her a spare key before leaving the house. He had a voice-over job in the West End now and would be out for a couple of hours at least.

Barbara returned to the box room and flopped on the small single bed. It was almost four o'clock and she felt exhausted after everything that had happened today.

When she woke up some time later, she was briefly confused until she remembered where she was. Then, picking up her laptop, she went downstairs and back to the kitchen. The room was warm and cosy even though there was no one there. An old dresser stood against one wall and there were red cushions on pine chairs round a scrubbed pine table.

Barbara made herself another cup of tea and was about to check her emails when she noticed several cards lined up along a shelf. They were mainly invitations to film premieres and private views. One in particular caught her eye and she took it down to read.

Darling Alan,
I'd adore working with you again. If anyone can persuade her, you can. The party is on for next Friday – a big surprise for her birthday. Everyone will be there.
Love and kisses,
Felicity

There was a folded sheet of paper tucked inside the card and Barbara couldn't resist opening it. A small black-and-white photograph fell to the floor. When she picked it up, she saw it showed a group of people in Victorian costume. She was amazed to recognize Alan in a butler's uniform. The sheet of paper was headed 'To all the cast'. It read:

As you know, we have often discussed bringing the series back. Two weeks ago I had a meeting with a producer who expressed terrific interest. He said they would consider it, but

only if Margaret Reynolds agreed to be part of the cast. I know we were all saddened when she left, and her departure did, in the end, cause the series to finish. Could we persuade her? It would be so wonderful. They won't consider the show without her, so let's hope enough time has passed.
Felicity

Barbara was a good enough journalist to know there was a story here. Opening her laptop, she went immediately to Google and typed in 'Margaret Reynolds'. She faintly recalled the name but had no idea why.

A second or two later, everything fell into place. Margaret Reynolds had started her career as a stage actress with the National Theatre and the Royal Shakespeare Company. She had then gone on to star in *Harwood House*, a long-running television series. It had started in the late 1990s and achieved the highest viewing figures of any period drama. Photographs showed a very attractive dark-eyed woman. There were rave reviews of her playing Lady Helen Montague, the tortured heiress of Harwood House.

It seemed that the actress had married a leading French film actor called Armande

Dupont in a private ceremony. There were many pictures of the beautiful couple. But tragedy struck and he died in a helicopter crash two years after the wedding. A famous photograph showed Margaret holding up a hand to shield her face from the camera. One report stated that she'd collapsed on set while filming. Then came a series of screaming tabloid headlines:

'Further Heartbreak as Star Loses Baby'
'Actress Attempts Suicide'
'More Tragedy for Star as TV Series Folds'

Barbara read on and pieced together the story. Clearly Margaret had left *Harwood House* after her miscarriage and suicide attempt. Viewing figures dropped week by week. Finally, to the sadness of all the cast, the show was taken off.

Barbara slammed shut her laptop and rang Mike Phillips. Even though he had just sacked her, this was too good an opportunity to miss.

When Mike answered her call, he sounded surprised. He started to remind her that she no longer worked for the magazine, but Barbara interrupted him.

'Listen, Mike, what if I could get hold of

Margaret Reynolds? She's the star from *Harwood House*. I may be able to come up with some inside information about the BBC bringing back the show.'

Mike hesitated and then said, 'If you get some good material I might consider it. Only "might", mind you.'

'It could really be an amazing opening to my "Where Are They Now?" series. I could email you the list of all the other stars—'

Mike stopped Barbara, telling her to produce the Margaret Reynolds piece first.

'I've got Kevin Shorter to do the photographs,' Barbara went on.

'Well, he's one of the best. Let me know how it pans out and I'll make a final decision.'

When she put down the phone Barbara was flushed with excitement. She could already imagine herself winning an award for Journalist of the Year. The fact that she had not contacted Margaret Reynolds yet, and didn't even know where the woman lived, was not important.

She began to plan exactly how she would persuade Alan to take her to the surprise party.

Chapter Two

Alan came home a little later with a Chinese takeaway for both of them. He laid out all the different cartons in the kitchen: crispy duck and pancakes, sweet and sour pork, chicken with noodles. As he was taking plates from the dresser, Barbara smiled and then clapped her hands.

'Of course, Alan! I recognize you now. It's been bugging me since I got here.'

Alan said nothing. Instead he opened a bottle of wine and handed Barbara a glass.

'Weren't you the butler in that series . . . Now, what was it called? It was brilliant.'

'You mean *Harwood House*?'

'Yes! You were a butler and that amazing actress, what was her name . . . was it Margaret something?'

'Yes, Margaret Reynolds. But that was over five years ago.'

'No! Surely not five years?'

Alan offered her chopsticks so she could help herself to the food.

'Yes. And it's funny you should mention that show and Margaret now. A few of the cast are arranging a surprise party for her.'

'Oh, how extraordinary. I was such a fan and you were so good.'

Barbara ate hungrily as Alan described how the show had ended and what had happened to Margaret. No sooner than she had dealt with the loss of her gorgeous husband her sister died in a car crash.

Barbara made all the right noises. The more she heard, the better it sounded for her article.

Alan was flattered by all the attention. After dinner he showed Barbara a scrapbook of photographs and reviews of him in many different roles. In fact, it was all rather boring for Barbara. She had to be very careful not to put too much emphasis on *Harwood House* and Margaret Reynolds.

Luckily, Alan made things easy for her. He picked up the letter that Barbara had already read.

'I got this last week. It's from Felicity Wright, who was an actress in the show. Just imagine, Felicity and her husband bought an old cottage in Kent and now she's seen Margaret in the village.'

'Good heavens,' Barbara exclaimed. 'What a coincidence.'

Alan nodded.

'She keeps a very low profile. Felicity doesn't think anyone in the village even knows who Margaret is. She took over some huge manor house that belonged to her sister. She's a recluse and lives on her own. Actually, Felicity has asked everyone to this surprise party she's arranging in the country. Margaret will be there. There's a plan to maybe revive the show.'

By now they'd finished the bottle of wine between them and Alan was starting to yawn. Barbara was desperate to keep him talking, so she asked if he'd like a cup of coffee.

She hoped that Alan would continue, but instead he sighed and said, 'Well, I need to get to my bed. Just help yourself to coffee or anything you want.'

Barbara was woken by Alan tapping on her bedroom door.

'I've got an early start today. I'll be home this afternoon. You'll probably be out flat-hunting, I imagine.'

Barbara hoped he wasn't having second thoughts about her staying. She smiled sweetly and said, 'Oh yes. I've got a few flats to see today.'

'Good luck, then. There's coffee already made.'

She waited to hear the front door close

before she went down to the kitchen. As she was helping herself to coffee, the phone rang and the answer machine clicked on.

'Hi, Alan. It's me, Felicity. I'm at the cottage. Guess what? Last night I saw Margaret at the local petrol station. I'm afraid I let the cat out of the bag.'

Barbara snatched up the phone.

'Hello. Alan will be out all day. Is it something important?'

'Er, not really. I'll call his mobile.'

'He won't have it turned on. He's recording. I'm Barbara, a close friend. Is this about Margaret Reynolds? I know he's looking forward to seeing her again.'

'Oh, we all are.' Felicity sounded hesitant, but then continued, 'Will you tell him that we are going to meet for a drink first at the Hare and Hounds at about seven? The numbers have grown and it's not that much of a surprise. Margaret suggested we have the get-together at her house.'

'I'll tell him.'

Felicity hung up and Barbara deleted the message.

Barbara spent the day doing more research on Margaret Reynolds. She had just closed her laptop when Alan drew up in his car.

'Hi. Any luck?' he asked as he came into the kitchen.

For a minute Barbara thought he was referring to Margaret Reynolds and she nodded. Then she realized that he was talking about a new place for her to live. Thinking quickly, she pretended to be quite keen on a flat share and said she hoped to meet the owner next week.

'So you'll be here for the weekend?'

Round-eyed, Barbara put her hand to her mouth like a child and said, 'Oh, is that all right?'

'Well ...' Alan paused, as if unsure how to answer. Finally, he said, 'Yes, of course. No problem.'

As Alan hung up his coat, Barbara said, 'By the way, there was a call for you. I answered because I thought it might be my editor. It was Felicity.'

Barbara gave him the message and then added, 'I hope you don't mind. She sounded so sweet. When I said I was such a fan of the show, she suggested that maybe I'd like to go with you.'

'What, to Kent?'

'Yes. I was so thrilled.'

'Did she leave a number?'

'No. She said she was at her cottage.'
Alan shrugged.
'Well, if she said it's OK.'
Barbara threw her arms around him.
'Oh, thank you, Alan.'

Chapter Three

On Friday, Barbara did try to help Alan, but he was so capable she just felt in the way. He had made lots of food for the party and in no time everything was packed into plastic containers. He hardly said a word to Barbara while he worked. She hoped this was because he was so busy, but she had a nasty feeling he was getting rather fed up with her.

It was true that Alan was beginning to wonder if Barbara would ever leave. She seemed to be making no real effort to find somewhere new to live. To make matters worse, this morning she'd tinted her hair in the bathroom and stained a towel. There were now drips the colour of blood on the tiled floor.

When Barbara rather nervously asked if she should dress up or make it casual, he snapped, 'Wear anything you feel comfortable in.'

Barbara chose a short plaid skirt, black stockings, boots and a black polo-necked sweater. She also wore big gold earrings and matching bangles. Alan had on a very smart navy velvet suit and a white collarless shirt.

'Do I look all right?' Barbara asked.

He gave her a glance and shrugged.

'Sure. We should get started.'

After driving in silence for about half an hour, Alan gradually became less tense.

'I think I should make something clear, Barbara.'

'Fire away.'

'OK, this is a get-together of old mates and cast members for Margaret's birthday. But there is an ulterior motive.'

'Really?' she said innocently.

'Yeah, we want her to come back into the show. Some of us haven't had much work recently and it would be a big plus for all of us. So, everything I've told you is private, understand? Off the record. I just feel rather nervous.'

'About what?'

'Well, I know you're intending doing this gig with Kevin, finding ex-soap stars.'

'Oh, for heaven's sake, Alan, you couldn't describe your series as a soap. It was a very serious drama.' By this time Barbara was being such a creep she was even making herself feel a bit sick.

'No, no, I know that. But I don't want you trying to hassle Margaret. Promise me that whatever happens tonight is off the record.'

Barbara nodded and then patted Alan's shoulder.

'I promise, but you didn't even need to bring it up. I'm so thrilled to be meeting her and the rest of the brilliant cast.'

Just as Alan and Barbara pulled in at the Hare and Hounds, three actors from the show arrived. There was a lot of chit-chat about who was doing what, or not doing anything at all. Barbara remained very much in the background, behaving herself, not that she recognized anyone.

Felicity arrived to whoops and a lot of air-kissing. She suggested that they go in convoy to Margaret's house as she knew the way and so, after a drink, everyone got into various cars to follow her ancient Mini.

They left the main road and drove along a series of increasingly narrow lanes. By the end, they appeared to be heading towards a dirt track.

'This can't be right,' Alan muttered as they bounced over a number of potholes.

Eventually they reached a steep embankment.

There were now thick woods on either side of them. Suddenly a lightning bolt zigzagged across the sky, followed quickly by a crash of thunder. As Felicity stopped her car at a sign and got out to look at it more closely, the rain started lashing down.

She waved to the next car and shouted, 'This is it.'

'I hope she's right,' Alan groaned.

The convoy rounded a bend that was lined by tall fir trees. They stopped at a white-painted gate with a postbox on the top bar. Felicity had to get out of her car again to open the gate and was soaked by the time she'd finished.

'It's straight ahead from here,' she shouted.

They moved on to a tarmac road that was a lot easier to drive along than the track. As they went round another bend the old manor house came into view. Even though it was dark, they could make out a huge Victorian building with turrets at either end. Strange-looking stone creatures flanked the main entrance. There were big bay windows on the ground floor, some dark but others well lit. There were also three cars parked at the top of the horseshoe-shaped drive: an old Land Rover and two BMWs.

'That belongs to James Halliday, the show's producer,' Alan said, pointing towards one of the BMWs.

Barbara nodded, trying not to seem too interested. 'Looks like we've enough food for a banquet,' she said, watching as everyone gathered, arms laden, on the stone steps leading to the door.

Felicity pulled the old iron bell, which clanged loudly and ominously. Eventually they heard footsteps.

The door was swung open by James Halliday, the producer. He was portly, with thinning hair, and was dressed in a flamboyant floral shirt. He flung out his arms and bellowed, 'Welcome.'

There were a lot of 'hellos' and 'darlings' and many cheeks were kissed. Then James directed everyone down a dark hall towards the kitchen. Off to one side they could just make out a wide staircase with a worn paint-spattered carpet. There was a chandelier with many bulbs missing, but the crystals glittered brightly.

Like everyone else, Barbara stepped gingerly in the dark, following James through big green-painted doors.

*

The kitchen was surprisingly bright, warm and welcoming. It had high glass-fronted cabinets, some half-stripped of their paint. They were filled with blue-and-white crockery. Dominating the huge space was a fifteen-foot oak table. Stacked at the far end were wine glasses and paper plates and big bowls of salad. One wall was taken up by a vast Aga. A log fire was blazing opposite. There was a large Chesterfield sofa with tartan rugs folded on the arms and velvet cushions scattered at the back.

Barbara emptied Alan's box of food and laid things out on plates. She was trying to make herself useful, as everyone else seemed to know each other and they were busy chattering away very loudly.

There was an uneasy atmosphere, all of them wondering where the star of the party was. Some whispered that she might not make an appearance. People were drinking and starting to pick at the food when Alan clapped his hands.

'Here she is.'

Margaret Reynolds stood in the doorway, even more beautiful than in the photographs. She had thick, dark, shoulder-length hair, flawless skin and large dark brown eyes. Her face, devoid of make-up, was very pale but her cheeks were flushed. She was also taller than Barbara had thought and very slender. She was wearing a high-collared Victorian blouse with a brooch at her neck and leg-of-mutton sleeves that were frilled at her wrists. Her long dark skirt was fitted to perfection, showing off her flat stomach and shapely hips.

They all grew silent and then Alan, rather embarrassingly, began to sing 'Happy Birthday'. Everyone joined in and Margaret accepted a glass of wine. She seemed deeply shy and her hand was shaking as she raised her glass. She had a lovely soft sweet voice.

'Thank you all for coming. Before the party really begins I think you should all know that, as much as I appreciate you making such an effort, there is no possibility of my returning to work on the series. I have already told our wonderful producer, James, that I have retired and there is nothing that will change my mind.'

She lifted the glass to her lips and sipped, as everyone began talking to cover their disappointment. Barbara was fascinated, watching as Margaret moved from one person to another.

Margaret caught sight of Barbara and headed towards her.

'I'm sorry, have we met before?'

'No, I'm a friend of Alan's.'

Alan quickly came over and made the introductions.

'Are you an actress, Barbara?'

'No, I'm a writer.'

Alan was obviously relieved that she hadn't said she was a journalist. Margaret moved off and Barbara leaned close to Alan.

'She's gorgeous, so beautiful.'

'Yes. And she doesn't seem to have aged at all.'

Barbara tried to mingle, but it wasn't easy. The actors all talked about old times and there were a few laughs as they recalled amusing things that had happened. Someone turned on the radio and found a music station. It was an improvement, but this was clearly not a very successful birthday party.

After several glasses of wine, Barbara needed the bathroom. She asked Felicity for directions and was pointed down the corridor, not far from the kitchen.

Barbara slipped out, but when she got there the door was locked. She waited for a while and then, glancing around, headed further down the hallway towards the front door. She looked up the wide staircase. The hallway was dark, lit only by a few candles and the old chandelier.

Barbara was suddenly eager to see inside some of the other rooms. One door creaked when she pushed it open, but no one seemed to be around. She peered in and saw a huge drawing room with all the furniture draped in dustsheets. She closed the door, wincing as it creaked loudly again.

She peered up the stairway to the floor above, then began to creep up the stairs. It was very dark, but eventually her eyes grew accustomed to it. She reached the first landing. The carpet was so threadbare she had to be careful not to trip. A door was ajar and she could see a four-poster bed with old green velvet drapes. Next to it was a big dressing table with make-up and bottles of perfume all over the surface.

Barbara closed the door and inched along the corridor. It was a little lighter here as there was a large window at the end through which the moon spread a cold white glow. She could make out a small door with a china doorknob covered in flowers. She turned the knob and the door opened on to a child's playroom. There were puzzles and games littering the floor. She noticed a cot with many dolls inside, as if in a small prison. Then she heard voices, so she quickly made her way back to the top of the stairs.

The front door was open now and some of the guests were leaving, laughing and calling out farewells. Barbara moved cautiously down the staircase.

She stopped. There was a strange click-clicking noise coming from behind her. She turned and saw a clockwork rabbit. Its fur was a dirty grey but its glass eyes shone brightly. It was hopping down each stair. As it somersaulted and gained the next step, the rabbit clapped its paws together. It had a distorted, slightly whirring, high-pitched voice that kept repeating the same phrase:

'Bunny bunny, hip hop.
Keep moving, don't stop.'

Two guests heard the mechanical voice and turned to look up the stairs. As soon as they spotted Barbara, the creature fell on its side and stopped singing.

'I was ... er ... looking for the lavatory,' Barbara said in an embarrassed voice.

And at that point she felt a really hard push

in the small of her back. Losing her balance, she tripped and fell head first down the stairs.

In seconds she had struck her head hard on the newel post and passed out.

Chapter Four

James Halliday carried Barbara into the kitchen and laid her down on the sofa. Alan put a cold cloth on her head and waited for her to come round. When she did, she explained how she'd tripped on a toy on the stairs. From the look on Alan's face, she had a feeling he didn't believe her.

Margaret had already called the local doctor. By the time he arrived, all the guests apart from Alan had left. The doctor strapped up Barbara's ankle, observing that it was quite a bad sprain. He suggested that Margaret monitor the situation. If the swelling got worse, Barbara would need to go to hospital for an X-ray. He prescribed painkillers for her ankle and suggested that they use hot and cold compresses to help the swelling go down.

Barbara closed her eyes. She hadn't told anyone about being pushed. Had she just had too much to drink and imagined it? Maybe it was the noise of the clockwork rabbit hopping down the stairs that had startled her and made her lose her footing.

Alan came to sit beside her. He was concerned, but at the same time he couldn't help wondering if Barbara had planned this in order to spend a night in the house.

'Listen, Margaret has kindly said you can stay over. It's a long drive and you are obviously not in good shape.'

Barbara liked the idea more than he could know. She smiled weakly.

'That's awfully nice of her, if it's not too much trouble.'

Margaret came across and sat by the sofa. 'You can stay down here in the kitchen,' she told Barbara. 'I'll build up the fire so you will be nice and warm.'

'I really don't want to make a fuss,' Barbara said, sounding pathetic.

Alan was torn. On the one hand he didn't quite trust Barbara, but on the other he was worried about getting back to London because he had an early start in the morning.

After a few minutes' thought he said, 'How would it be if I call tomorrow from London to arrange when I can collect you?'

Barbara nodded and watched as Margaret and Alan went out into the hall.

She then eased herself up. Her ankle did hurt,

a little, and she did have a slight headache, but she could easily have gone back with Alan. However, this was a great opportunity to get more information on Margaret.

When Margaret returned, Barbara closed her eyes, pretending to be asleep. She could hear her moving around the kitchen, clearing up. Margaret must then have picked up a big thick blanket, because Barbara could feel it being gently laid over her. She opened her eyes and gave a weak smile.

'Thank you so much. I'm sorry for the inconvenience.'

'That's all right. I am very happy that you are here. There is a lavatory in the hall just on the left. If you need me during the night, there's the old bell-pull near the stove. Is there anything you would like?'

'No, thank you.'

'Goodnight, then,' said Margaret, closing the door behind her.

Barbara sat up and looked around. It was so warm and cosy in here, if a bit shabby. She listened but could hear nothing. Easing back the blanket, she slowly placed her feet on the stone-flagged floor. Her ankle was slightly swollen, but it really didn't hurt. She stood up and made her way towards the pantry. Shivering, she helped herself to a couple of sausage rolls. Then she carried them back to the old sofa and drew the blanket around herself.

Barbara must have dozed off, because the fire was much lower when she was woken by the tink-tink-tink of a piano being played, the same notes over and over again. Sitting up, she thought she could hear muffled voices. Was Margaret talking to someone? The piano stopped and then there was silence. She assumed someone else must have stayed over upstairs.

Barbara was woken again by the sound of scraping. Margaret was clearing the grate and making up a fresh fire with big logs and coals. There was a wonderful smell of coffee and bacon.

'Good morning, Barbara.' Margaret leaned over her and gently touched her shoulder. 'How are you feeling?'

'So much better. I slept really well.'

'Yes. It's a comfortable old Chesterfield. I'm making breakfast. Are you hungry?'

'Yes, I am.'

Barbara sat up and eased her legs round. Her ankle didn't hurt at all, but she winced as if in pain. She then made a big show of hopping on one foot, gripping the back of a chair before sitting at the table.

'I thought I heard you playing the piano last night,' Barbara said.

Margaret turned from the Aga, shaking her head.

'You must have been mistaken.'

'It seemed to come from upstairs.'

Shaking her head again, Margaret turned the bacon.

'How do you like your eggs?'

'Sunny side up, please,' Barbara said, helping herself to a slice of toast.

Margaret served breakfast, then asked Barbara if she thought she should be checked over by the hospital.

Barbara shook her head. 'I'm sure I'll be OK. I'll call Alan and ask him to collect me.' She paused. 'You have a lovely house.'

'It was my sister's,' said Margaret. 'She was intending to do it up and then convert it into separate apartments. She planned to sell each of them off and make a large profit. There are three floors. It's a Gothic monster.'

'That's a big project to take on.'

'Yes, it certainly is. There are also ten acres and a wooded copse behind the house which makes it quite dark. Most of the rooms are closed off, but I will get round to doing something with them one of these days.'

'How long have you lived here?'

Margaret wiped her lips with a linen napkin.

'Since my sister died.'

She pushed her chair back as if she didn't want to discuss it any further and said, 'I'm going to feed the birds.'

Barbara was left alone, sitting at the table. She'd cleaned her plate, even wiping it with some more toast, and had had two cups of coffee. Now she felt she should start to question Margaret more closely. But it wasn't going to be easy.

She decided to act friendly and not push for any details. She was very good at teasing out information from people, but time would be against her. If Alan was going to come and collect her soon, she didn't have very long.

She crossed to a window and looked out. A child's swing hung from the branches of a massive sprawling oak tree. She saw Margaret shiver, no doubt reacting to the change in temperature.

Barbara went to her handbag and took out her mobile phone. She called Alan but just got his voicemail. She left a message saying that her ankle was very swollen and she could hardly walk but would try him later. Margaret came in just as she was finishing.

'Alan's busy doing a voice-over, so he's not sure when he can come. Is there a train I could catch?'

Margaret said she wouldn't hear of it until Barbara's ankle was 100 per cent better.

Barbara thanked her, but then said, 'Do you know, a strange thing happened last night. I saw a clockwork rabbit hopping from stair to stair.'

Margaret smiled, but made no reply. Instead she said, 'I'm thinking of making an Irish stew. Would you like that?'

She went to help Barbara sit back on the sofa.

'I use lots of fresh vegetables with the lamb and potatoes. I let them simmer for a couple of hours.'

'Sounds delicious . . .'

'Of course, I'm nowhere near as good a cook as my husband was.'

'Your husband was French, wasn't he?'

Margaret nodded and went to a dresser. She opened a drawer and took out a framed picture.

'This is Armande. He was an actor.'

Barbara looked at the stunningly handsome dark-eyed man. He was in period costume, wearing a frilled shirt with a velvet waistcoat and tight-fitting trousers with riding boots.

'Gosh, he's so good-looking.'

'Yes. He was also a genuine, kind, loving man. I fell in love with him as soon as we met. He was everything I could ever have hoped for. He proposed to me after only a few months.'

Barbara made all the right noises as Margaret showed her more photographs. This time they were arranged in albums. There were lots of pictures of the two of them on their wedding day. They were not only a breathtakingly beautiful pair, but they were also obviously very much in love.

Barbara sighed. 'I've always dreamed of meeting someone like him. I seem to have a wretched ability to go for the wrong type. I've been constantly let down. In fact, only recently . . .'

Suddenly she felt tearful and found herself explaining how, in the last few days, she had been dumped by her boyfriend, lost her job and then been told to leave by her landlady. The only good thing was how kind Alan had been in allowing her to stay.

'What work do you do?'

Whoops! Barbara sniffed and blew her nose.

She was clever enough to think quickly and repeated that she was a writer.

'What kind of writing?' Margaret persisted.

'Oh, novels, though I haven't had any published yet.'

'I write,' Margaret said, smiling. 'Well, I want to write. I think I have a strong story, but I've never managed to get it down.'

'Maybe we can discuss it,' said Barbara with interest. 'If I can help at all, I'd love to be able to repay your kindness.'

Margaret closed her albums and looked thoughtful before saying, 'Maybe one day I'll be able to tell someone. Not right now. But I just keep thinking that if I were to write it down I would feel better.'

'Is it to do with no longer working as an actress?'

Margaret gave her a cool glance.

'No. My career is of no interest.'

She put the albums back in the drawer and closed it, before heading to the Aga to prepare the stew.

'Your husband died, didn't he?'

Again the cold glance.

'Yes. I couldn't write about that. If I think about it, I get so emotional I can hardly function. All that would happen is the pain would return. The memory of the day I was told Armande had died still burns inside me. Sometimes I wake at night and I live through it all over again. It was so hard to believe that he would never take me in his arms again. Never kiss me. Knowing I was never going to see him again, it felt as if I'd been swallowed by a whale.'

'A whale?'

Margaret suddenly gave an infectious childlike giggle.

'That's how I explained it to my therapist. I felt I was trapped inside a whale, swilling around with the water and the dead fish. I was unable to get out, always in the dark and yet warm. Every time the whale opened its massive jaws I tried. I thought that if I could just swim out to safety, Armande would still be alive.'

She had a puzzled expression on her beautiful face. No longer aware of how attentive Barbara was, she appeared to have moved into a world of her own. Her eyes closed and she remained silent.

Finally, Barbara said, 'Did you ever get out from the belly of the whale?'

Margaret's manner changed suddenly. Now angry, she clenched her fists.

'I didn't want to get out! I didn't want to

break through the heat and escape out through its jaws, because then I would be alive. In its belly I was dying.'

She gave another odd laugh, shaking her head.

'I was sent to a mental hospital. My sister arranged it. Ghastly place. I suppose I did swim out of its belly, because I was only there for a few months. I went back to work.'

She turned to her pan, picked up a big wooden spoon and stirred the contents.

'Did you feel you came to terms with the death of your husband?'

Margaret waved the spoon as she spoke.

'No. He was the love of my life. Until I'm buried beside him, the pain will continue. I exist because I have to. That is, until I can join him.'

'Have you ever contemplated suicide?'

'It's impossible for me to do that.'

Margaret seasoned and stirred the stew, then tasted it and smiled.

'Mmm . . . that's good. A bit more salt, then I'll leave it simmering.' She paused for a while before saying, 'It's going to snow. I can always tell. The clouds are dark and full. I do love a stew on a cold wintry day.'

'I should get dressed,' Barbara said.

'You don't have to if you don't want. You can rest up and maybe after lunch see how you feel. I have to run a few errands in the village.'

The sound of the phone, which was mounted on a wall in the kitchen, startled them both.

Margaret answered, then turned to Barbara.

'It's the doctor, enquiring how you're feeling. Do you want to talk to him?'

'Thank you,' Barbara said, and hobbled to the receiver.

She then explained that her ankle was still painful but the swelling had gone down considerably. There was, the doctor agreed, no need for her to go to hospital.

The two women were silent for a while, then Margaret spoke.

'The phone has such a loud ring because it's the only one in the house. This way, if I'm upstairs I can hear it.'

'Don't you have a mobile?' Barbara asked.

'No. I don't suppose you've noticed, but there is no television either.'

Barbara was surprised.

'Don't you feel lonely out here on your own?'

'No, I'm never lonely. Are you?'

Barbara was taken aback, but before she

could reply Margaret left the kitchen. Alone now, she pondered the question. She'd never really considered what she felt about her life. She was miserable a lot of the time, that was certainly true. And she was telling the truth about wanting to write, though she didn't have a clue what kind of novel. She sighed. If she was honest, she could hardly remember a time when she hadn't felt lonely.

Chapter Five

As soon as Margaret had driven off, Barbara wasted no time in dressing. She was eager to look over the house in daylight. She headed for the stairs and reached the first landing without any problems. She tried the door of the bedroom she'd looked into the night before. It was locked. She moved from one door to the next, but they were all locked.

Even though it was morning, it was still dark up here. When she switched on a landing light, it was dead. Moving cautiously back towards the stairs, she heard an odd sound in one of the rooms, like something hitting a wooden floor. She thought at first it must be the old central-heating pipes. But they would have made a clang, while this sounded more like a thud.

She moved to the locked door and touched the handle. It was cold and as she pulled her hand away the noise stopped. Completely puzzled and unnerved, she headed back to the kitchen.

Once there, Barbara gave the stew a good stir and decided to set the table. She found the dinner plates and started to hunt for knives and forks. While opening drawers, she came across Margaret's photograph albums.

She listened carefully to hear if the car was returning. It wasn't. So she lifted out the albums and flicked through one after another. The second album contained pictures of a pretty dark-haired woman who resembled Margaret. On the back of one of them was written 'Julia in Hastings'. There were also several pictures of a gorgeous blonde-haired little girl.

Barbara took four or five loose photographs and put them into her handbag.

She gave the stew another stir and was just replacing the lid when she heard the sound of the Land Rover returning.

Margaret came in the back way. Her cheeks were a rosy red and she had flecks of snow on her shoulders.

'I said it would snow. It's really coming down heavily now,' she said, placing her shopping bags on the kitchen counter. 'It's very cold out there. I think it may settle. We'll have such fun.'

She suddenly stopped, as if realizing for the first time that Barbara was there.

'Sorry. I get so used to talking to myself,' she said, and gave a light, soft giggle.

She took off her coat, shook it and rested it over the back of a kitchen chair.

'Oh, you've set the table too. How nice of you.'

Margaret removed her wellington boots and woolly hat, running her hands through her long hair. She then went over to the Aga and gave the stew a taste.

'Mmm, I'm hungry. Let's have lunch early.'

She fetched a bottle of wine and opened it.

'Screw tops! Cheap plonk. How things change . . . no more corks.'

Margaret was so bubbly and friendly, Barbara couldn't help but enjoy her company.

Barbara was also surprised to find herself more than ready to eat lunch, even though she'd already had a cooked breakfast. She usually ate sandwiches or takeaways and very rarely a proper meal. Today, though, she felt starving.

They sat at the old oak table. The stew was delicious and Barbara had two helpings. They had cheese and biscuits to follow. Between them they drank the whole bottle of red plonk before washing the dishes together.

Margaret made a fresh pot of coffee and they were sitting beside the blazing fire when she suddenly jumped up.

'Look! Look outside!'

The snow had indeed settled into a thick sheet and was covering the ground like a soft white blanket.

'This will last, I'm sure. The roads were already icy when I went out. Good job I restocked when I did. Last winter I was frozen in here for over ten days.'

She suddenly put her hand to her mouth.

'Oh, my goodness. We'd better call Alan. He'll have to set off straight away if he wants to collect you.'

Barbara took out her mobile, dialled and waited. Alan was still on voicemail.

'Maybe I should get a train,' she suggested half-heartedly.

'Certainly not. But your ankle does seem to be better. You've stopped limping, I see.' Margaret gave an odd half-smile, as if she knew Barbara had been lying.

'Is there a local taxi that could take me to the station?'

Margaret checked an old notebook hanging on a piece of string by the phone.

'I have a few numbers. Let me call the station first and see what times the trains are running to London.'

She looked up, smiling.

43

'If the worst comes to the worst, I can drive you.'

Margaret discovered there was a direct train at five fifteen, but the local taxi service was engaged.

'You could stay on here. Do you have something to get back to London for?' Margaret asked.

'I don't actually. I was going to look for a place to live,' Barbara replied.

Margaret placed more logs on to the fire, making a really big blaze. The kitchen was as warm as toast.

'Do you play Scrabble?' she asked, as she opened a wooden box and delved inside.

'Yes, I do.'

'Shall we have a game?'

Margaret opened the board and with childish enthusiasm began counting out the letters. Then she looked up, listening.

'The wind is picking up. It howls round the house. Always sounds a lot worse than it is. Everything rattles.'

They played for over an hour. Margaret was very competitive and won every game. She called the taxi company again, but they were booked out for the afternoon.

'Maybe we shouldn't even think about your

leaving today. I can fix up a bedroom for you, or you can stay down here as it's so warm.'

Barbara didn't hesitate. Another evening, another chance to gather more information.

'I'll stay over if you don't mind.'

Margaret patted Barbara's cheek.

'Of course I don't mind. In fact, I'm really enjoying your company. I like you.'

'I like you too,' Barbara said.

She blushed when Margaret caught hold of her hand and kissed her fingers.

'I need a friend. Are you going to be a friend, Barbara?'

Barbara paused and then said softly, 'I would like to be your friend.'

Chapter Six

It grew dark quickly that afternoon and the snow never stopped falling.

Margaret said she would go and check upstairs. She wanted to make sure that the plumbing was behaving itself.

'I won't be long. Sometimes the pipes get frozen if I don't run the hot water.'

Barbara was disconcerted to realize that Margaret had locked the kitchen door after she left.

The phone rang, breaking into the silence. It was Alan. Barbara explained she would be staying over another night because of the snow. Alan was relieved, as he didn't feel like driving to collect her.

'Just don't go nosing around. She's a very private lady,' he warned, and rang off.

The old house creaked and moaned. Barbara could hear the rattle of pipes, but then she heard something else.

'Stay in your room and behave yourself, do you hear me?'

Barbara sat bolt upright. There were running footsteps, followed by silence. She was startled when the key turned in the locked kitchen door.

Margaret came in looking very agitated and pocketed the key.

'Is everything all right?' Barbara asked.

'Yes. Why wouldn't it be?' Margaret snapped, then she began to bang around the kitchen, preparing supper. Her radical mood change was unnerving.

Sitting by the fire as Margaret busied herself cooking, Barbara was certain she heard soft footsteps running above her. She wondered again if there was someone else in the house. Was it the person who had pushed her down the stairs?

'Sometimes in old houses you hear strange noises,' she ventured.

'It's the hot-water pipes,' Margaret said sharply.

Again the footsteps sounded above her and Barbara looked up to the ceiling. There was an old slatted wooden airer, with a rope attached. It was shaking, just a fraction.

'Watch the rice for me. I won't be a minute,' Margaret said, then hurried out.

Barbara pressed her ear against the locked

door. She distinctly heard Margaret running up the stairs. She could also hear her talking, but could not make out what she was saying. Then came lighter steps and a door slamming shut. She only just made it back to the armchair by the fire before Margaret returned.

For a moment there was silence, then both of them were aware of a hissing noise coming from the Aga.

'You didn't check on the rice,' Margaret said angrily, taking the pan to the sink.

'I'm so sorry. Let me clean up.'

'No, I'm doing it.'

Barbara sat back in the chair. She was beginning to think that perhaps there was something wrong with her host. She was so hostile all of a sudden.

'I need to use the bathroom,' Barbara said, standing up.

'Use the one on this floor, please, and check the water flushes properly when you pull the chain.'

Barbara made her way into the dark hall. Just as she was opening the door to the bathroom she heard the click-click and then the high-pitched song:

'Bunny bunny, hip hop.
Keep moving, don't stop.'

It was the clockwork rabbit, slowly hopping from one stair to the next. The toy gradually wound down and fell on its side. Its high-pitched voice became distorted as it repeated 'hop, hop, hop'.

Barbara picked up the rabbit. It was worn in places. Its ears were minus bits of fur and its white tail was decidedly the worse for wear. It was also heavier than she'd expected. It had a frilly blue dress with a tear where the key poked through.

Barbara went into the lavatory and stood the rabbit on the floor. Its bright beady eyes looked at her and it held up its front paws as if ready to dance. After flushing as instructed, Barbara returned to the kitchen with the rabbit.

'Look what I found on the stairs,' she said.

Margaret dropped the glass bowl in her hands. It broke into a hundred pieces on the stone-flagged floor. She snatched the rabbit from Barbara's hands and ran out of the kitchen.

Barbara could hear her footsteps on the landing. Doors slammed and there was shouting.

Not sure what to do, she found a brush and pan and swept up the broken glass. As she tipped the pieces into the bin, Margaret came back. Her cheeks were flushed and she was obviously distressed.

'Are you all right?' Barbara asked.

'No, I'm not, but please don't talk to me. I have to go out for a while.'

Margaret grabbed her big coat and, even though it was snowing heavily, she went out into the garden. From the window Barbara could see her, standing with her back to the house, hunched up. She was clearly crying, because her shoulders were heaving up and down.

Barbara fetched her own coat. Buttoning it up against the chill, she went out to join Margaret.

'Please, whatever is upsetting you, share it with me.'

'No. Leave me alone.'

'It's freezing out here. At least come back inside.'

'NO!'

Barbara put her arms around Margaret, who resisted at first but then leaned against her and started to speak.

'If you only knew how much I want to share what is happening in this house. But I can't. I'm so scared. If I tell you I would be sent back to that place. I'm not mad, I'm not. I so badly want it to end, but I promised.'

Barbara said nothing. She simply held her, until Margaret had calmed down, and then together they returned to the kitchen. She helped Margaret off with her wet coat and settled her into a chair by the fire.

Margaret sat staring into the flames, her hands clasped together. Her cheeks were flushed, her eyes bright with weeping, but she was calmer. Shaking her head, she apologized for the way she had behaved.

Barbara found a half-bottle of brandy and poured a big measure.

'Here, drink this. You must be so cold.'

'You have no idea how cold I am. Thank you.'

As Barbara busied herself finishing their supper, Margaret sat silently sipping her brandy. Barbara wondered again if there was someone else living in the upstairs rooms. It could be a mad relative. Perhaps they were violent ... Again she remembered that push down the stairs.

'Supper's ready,' she called a few minutes later.

Margaret slowly got up, placing her empty brandy glass on the table. Her shoulders sagged.

'It's probably not as good as you intended. I think the rice is overcooked,' Barbara said, serving out their meal.

Margaret gave a wan smile. She picked up her fork, took a small mouthful and poured herself a glass of wine. They continued to eat in silence, Margaret picking at her food but continuing to drink. Suddenly she focused her attention on Barbara.

'Tell me about your family.'

Barbara cocked her head to one side. She explained that there was not a lot to tell. She had been an only child, her mother falling pregnant in her late forties. Her parents were moderately wealthy and lived in a very comfortable house in Pinner, but her father had died when she was seven. His death had left her mother deeply depressed and unable to cope with a young daughter. She in turn had died when Barbara was thirteen.

'So I went to live with my aunt in Harrogate. I couldn't wait to leave Yorkshire. Then I lived in a horrible shared flat with six other students and I had to get work to supplement my college fees.'

Barbara had not been asked about her life before. Now, as she talked, she realized that she'd never had a loving relationship with anyone. To her astonishment, she started crying as a terrible wave of sadness swept over her.

From being the comforter, she became comforted as Margaret got up and put her arms around her.

Barbara sniffed and wiped her eyes on the napkin.

'I don't know why I'm crying. I seem to have done a lot of that lately. I've never really thought about what a non-existent family I had . . .'

'Do you want a family of your own?' Margaret asked, pouring more wine.

'Yes, I suppose so. It's just never been a choice I was in a position to make. I never met the right person like you did. '

'So you're all alone?'

Barbara drank her wine and nodded.

'Yes. I don't make friends that easily . . . maybe because I'm not a very nice person to be friends with.'

She started to cry again, on the verge of blurting out why she was there, when Margaret interrupted.

'I've had many friends. I have shut them out of my life. I think seeing so many of them at the party has just made it even more unbearable.'

'Why are you hiding yourself out here?'

Barbara wished she hadn't asked, as immediately Margaret tensed.

'If I was to tell you, you would not believe it.'

'Why don't you try? I'm a very good listener.'

Margaret gave a false laugh and rose from the table, stumbling.

'Whoops. I've had too much to drink. I need to go to bed. You will be all right sleeping down here again, won't you?'

'Of course. Leave all this to me.'

As Barbara cleared the table, Margaret paused and gave a sad smile before leaving the room.

Barbara began washing the dishes and stacking them on the draining board. It was still only eight o'clock. When she tried to find a programme on the radio it was full of static. She had finished the bottle of wine and was looking for something to read when Margaret walked in with a quilted dressing gown and a white cotton nightdress. Barbara jumped with fright.

'It's Victorian,' Margaret said. 'I used to collect them.'

She was wearing a similar high-necked nightdress, with an old velvet dressing gown.

In strained tones Margaret went on, 'Don't

worry if you hear noises. This old house creaks and groans, and with the snow on the roof you'll hear the pipes banging. If the snow melts, you'll hear it falling from the gutters. The generator is ancient and the lights often fail, so you might need these candles.'

Margaret had lit two candles in carved wooden candlesticks. Rattling a box of matches, she placed them on the table.

'Sometimes the house seems to have a mind all of its own.'

Barbara felt uneasy and asked Margaret not to lock the kitchen door in case she needed to use the bathroom. Margaret turned and paused. 'If you stay in the kitchen you'll be all right.'

Then she was gone.

Disturbed by this odd behaviour, Barbara was even more certain that there was someone else upstairs. The kitchen was warm, the fire was blazing, but the big room was full of shadows and strange shapes.

She washed her face in the kitchen sink, cleaned her teeth and changed into the nightdress. She was unfolding the blanket when she heard footsteps.

She expected Margaret to walk in, but nothing happened. She crossed the room and listened, easing the door open a fraction. It was pitch dark in the hall and there was a blast of freezing air. The further she opened the door, the colder it felt. By taking one small step into the hallway she could see that the front door was wide open.

Margaret was coming in. She had on a long cloak with a fur-lined hood and looked very angry. Afraid that she would be seen, Barbara pulled the door shut. She stayed by the fire for almost half an hour. Then she simply had to go and have a look.

The house was silent. By the light of the candle, Barbara crept out into the hall and went to the window by the front door. She peeked out. Another soft flurry of snow was sweeping over the driveway. Just as she was turning away she saw something that chilled her.

Footprints were plainly visible: not one set, but two. One was larger than the other. They were quite clear. Two people had been walking side by side. The prints led to a little snowman, about a foot high, with pebbles for eyes and a button for a nose.

'I was right. There is someone else in the house,' she whispered.

Barbara hurried back to the kitchen. She left

the candle burning as she thought about what she'd seen. Had Margaret had a child, one that was sick and needed to be locked up? Was this what she was so afraid of anyone finding out?

Barbara could feel herself dozing. She'd had a lot to drink. Why hadn't she brought her laptop, or anything on which she could write down what was happening? She really wanted to talk to her editor. This would make a fascinating article.

She fell into a deep sleep dreaming about her successful series, 'Where Are They Now?'. It featured sad, lonely Margaret Reynolds, who was destined to live out her life as a recluse to care for a sick child.

Chapter Seven

It was midnight and the kitchen was dark. From the dying embers of the fire came shadows that made eerie shapes on the walls.

The sound of a piano being played very badly woke her. Tink-tink-tink. Then there was the sound of the lid being banged shut. Next came the light running footsteps, like a child's. This was followed by Margaret's voice, muffled and indistinct, obviously having a conversation.

Barbara could hear a nursery rhyme, 'Three Blind Mice', repeated over and over again. She decided that she would go upstairs and see for herself.

She put on the dressing gown. Lighting her candle, she silently eased open the kitchen door. She crept along the hall and made her way upstairs. There was no sign of Margaret. She tried one of the other doors that had been locked. This time it opened.

A child's bedroom was painted pink, with a pink duvet and pillows. Nothing frightening whatsoever. The pink-and-white wardrobe was filled with velvet party frocks, patent-leather shoes, kilts and sweaters and blouses. Hats, coats and more shoes were lined up on one side.

Barbara had to hold her cupped hand to the flame, afraid it would splutter out or drip wax. She quietly closed the door, then froze. From above on the second floor she heard the same light footsteps. Someone hopping and skipping and then Margaret's voice, clearly this time.

'Stop it! Now just behave. You have to practise. I mean it, so do as I ask. DON'T TRY TO GET OUT! STOP IT! STOP IT!'

Barbara was afraid to go up to the next floor. The candle flame was low. It had burned right down to the rim of the candlestick.

The sound of the piano started again. Now it was even louder, as a duet began. 'Chopsticks'. Margaret must be playing too. Then came clapping and Margaret saying, 'Good. Very good. Now practise some more.'

Barbara made her way downstairs. She looked into the large drawing room with all the drapes over the furniture. She moved to the mantelpiece and held up the low flame of the candle to see better. There was a portrait above the fireplace, obviously of Margaret's sister. She had one hand resting on the arm of a chair.

The other held the hand of a small child who wore a white muslin dress. She had flaxen hair in lovely natural curls.

Holding the candle closer, Barbara tried to see the girl's face, only to almost drop the candlestick in shock. There was no face, just a shape of where it had been. Someone had painted it out.

The flame wavered and died as Barbara crept back to the kitchen, her heart thudding. She stacked up more logs to create a blaze, but her feet were freezing cold and she felt chilled to the bone. It was so cold she eventually took the cushions off the sofa and piled them in front of the fire.

Barbara woke with a start, her heart pounding. Margaret was rattling the grate and clearing out the ashes.

'You were dead to the world,' she said, smiling.

Barbara felt stiff all over and moaned as she stretched.

'Is your ankle hurting you?'

'Er, no. It's much better. Just a bit of cramp.'

'That's good. You do have a little bruise on your forehead.'

She touched Barbara's face gently, then

brightly suggested they have some bacon and eggs.

'It's stopped snowing and the sun looks as if it might come out,' she continued, sounding very happy.

Eating a full breakfast even though she didn't want it, Barbara was sure the 'happy' act was exactly that. Margaret looked tired, with dark circles beneath her eyes, and she was very pale. She hardly ate anything but chatted about how she wouldn't be able to function without her precious gas-fuelled Aga.

'I think I'll have a walk. Why don't you come to church with me? It's not far.'

Barbara refused, saying that it would not be a good idea in case she slipped, especially as her ankle was healing.

'I've left sweaters and a tracksuit with some underwear in the bathroom for you to use,' Margaret said, pulling on her wellingtons.

'Thank you. I really appreciate it. You're so kind.'

As soon as Margaret left, Barbara hurried up to the bathroom and ran the tap. The water was not that hot, but it was warm enough.

Dressed in a green sweater and the grey tracksuit left for her, Barbara made her way to the stairs leading up to the second floor. There was the same rather threadbare carpet. The sun streamed through the windows, making long shafts of light. Barbara peeked into two rooms that were clearly used for storage. At the end of the landing were double doors painted white with wooden doorknobs.

Barbara winced as the doors creaked loudly, then they swung open easily. They revealed stripped pine floors and a large blackboard with sticks of chalk held in a net bag. There were simple sums on the board. Around the walls were childish paintings in bright colours. A desk with a small chair was placed in front of the blackboard. Exercise books were stacked neatly beside a row of sharpened pencils. An upright piano was against a wall, music left open on the stand.

There was nothing frightening here, although it was a little strange. She went out and closed the door. Leading off the same corridor was another small winding staircase up to the third floor. There was a child's gate across the stairs. They were uncarpeted, but stained in whitewash that looked as if it had been done many years ago.

Barbara wondered if these stairs led up to whoever she suspected was living in the house.

Just as she was about to unhook the child's gate, she heard the sound of a car drawing up. She panicked and hurried back along the landing.

She ran downstairs and opened the front door just as the milkman was making his way down the drive. He turned and waved, apologizing for being late. Barbara smiled and bent to pick up the milk, but then she hesitated. The footsteps she'd seen the previous night had melted. The snowman was just a little pile of slush.

Returning to the kitchen, Barbara checked her mobile, but the battery flickered and she got no signal. Of course Margaret wouldn't have a charger. She tried the landline, but there was no connection.

It was strange to be so isolated. No mobile, no telephone, no television, no newspapers even. She couldn't remember a time when she'd been without these everyday things. No people, no contact with anyone apart from Margaret.

Surprisingly, she was beginning to like the feeling.

'I'm home,' Margaret called, coming into the kitchen with her cheeks rosy red once more.

She threw off her coat and warmed her hands in front of the fire.

'The trains will be running again tomorrow morning. There's one at ten that goes directly to Waterloo.'

She turned to Barbara, pulling off her hat, and added, 'I might come with you.'

'Oh, that would be nice.'

Margaret gave her a radiant smile.

'Yes. I have made some big decisions. First, I need to settle some important business.'

She pulled the big armchair closer to the fire.

'I talked to Alan this morning.'

Barbara began to feel worried.

'The vicar is such a sweetheart and let me use his phone. Anyway, I told Alan that you'd catch the train.'

'Oh, good.'

There was an awkward pause. Then Margaret said, 'I also spoke to Kevin. He's back earlier than he expected from his photoshoot.'

'Oh.'

'Yes. And he said that would mean it wasn't convenient for you to stay on any longer with them. He'd be grateful if you moved your things out.'

Barbara sank down on the sofa as Margaret went on.

'It's such a little house. I often went there for dinner with them. Such nice people, and very good cooks.'

'Yes.'

There was another pause.

Barbara began to wonder if Kevin had said something else.

'You're a journalist, aren't you?'

Barbara flushed.

'Er, yes, I am actually.'

'And you're planning to do a series about famous soap stars from the past, is that right?'

'Yes.'

'So you had an ulterior motive for coming here.'

'No, that isn't true.'

Margaret looked at her directly and Barbara couldn't meet her dark bright eyes.

'You want to write about me, don't you?'

'No, I really don't.'

Margaret gave a soft laugh, then said, 'I sort of suspected you were up to something.'

Barbara burst into tears.

'It's all right. Meeting James, Alan and the others that night made me even more certain. There is no way I could even think of returning to show business. The truth is, I never really fitted in. I did enjoy the fame for a while, but then it was hideous and intrusive. Losing Armande and then my sister and . . .'

She stopped and sighed deeply.

Barbara wiped her face with the back of her hand. She felt dreadful. She didn't know what to do or say.

'I'm so sorry.'

Margaret went to fill the kettle.

'Margaret, I'm really sorry to have lied to you. I'll leave tomorrow. And I promise I won't even consider writing anything. I have never known anyone like you. You have been so kind.'

'Good. I was hoping you'd say that.'

Margaret put the kettle on to the hot plate of the Aga.

'Do you like it here?' she asked, fetching the teapot.

Barbara went over to her, wanting more than anything to put her arms around her.

'I do. I really do. Just before you came in, I was thinking how comfortable I felt.'

Margaret patted her cheek.

'I know you have no work and no place to live, so it's perfect that you like it here. Maybe you could even begin to write that book.'

She opened a drawer and took out an old Bible, which she placed on the table.

'This belonged to my sister Julia.'

The air in the room grew charged as Margaret stared at Barbara.

'I want you to put your hand on it, because I'm going to tell you things that no one else has ever heard.'

Margaret caught Barbara's hand and held it tightly.

'What I'm going to tell you must never be repeated. If you swear to do this in good faith, then your promise is binding.'

'I promise. I won't ever write about you, I swear.'

'No, it's much more than that. What I'm going to tell you will frighten you. It's about this house. You might think I'm crazy, but I know you feel it. When you know it all, you will have to swear never to tell another living soul.'

'I'll do it, I'll swear.'

'Not yet. Tonight. We'll do it tonight.'

'Let me do it now.'

Margaret released her hand and picked up the Bible.

'But you haven't been told the secret yet. You don't know what you will be swearing to do. You'll have to wait until tonight.'

Chapter Eight

Barbara felt impatient, but Margaret happily busied herself for the rest of the afternoon preparing a fish pie. She was transformed, singing, turning the radio on and finding a programme with old music-hall songs. She even danced around the kitchen at one point. She was obviously not concerned about Barbara's background as a journalist.

Margaret then announced she would need to do some paperwork. Sitting at the kitchen table, she put on a pair of glasses and tackled a pile of documents. Every so often she would tear up something that appeared to annoy her. Then she would turn to a small notebook and write copious notes.

Barbara offered to make a pot of tea, but Margaret shook her head.

'I need to have everything ready for tomorrow.'

Finally Margaret stacked the papers she'd been working on into a pile and tossed everything she'd torn up on the fire. Then she put the fish pie in the oven.

'I'll come down at seven and we'll eat supper together. You can open a bottle of wine.'

'We are going to talk this evening, aren't we?'

Margaret turned at the kitchen door.

'Yes, of course.'

She gave a wide smile.

'I can't tell you what this means to me. It's such a relief. I haven't felt so at peace for years.'

Barbara was left to contemplate the burning papers in the grate. They looked like legal documents of some kind, but the flames blackened them before she could make out exactly what they were.

She checked the fish pie in the oven. She tried to read. Eventually she opened a bottle of wine and helped herself to a glass. She was sipping it when she saw Margaret's notebook left on the table. She hesitated, but couldn't resist opening it.

There were pages of lists. How to light the Aga if it went out. How to check on the central heating, the hot water and washing machine. When to pay the milkman. Underlined was how to turn the electric generator back on when the lights failed. Then, rather confusingly, came notes on homework: spelling tests, sums, multiplication tables and where to find atlases and encyclopedias.

Bored, Barbara helped herself to some more wine and tore a few blank pages from Margaret's notebook. She started to jot down a rough outline of the article for her editor. The more notes she made, the more she wondered just how unstable Margaret was and what the evening would bring.

At seven, the kitchen door banged open and Margaret hurried in. Barbara quickly stuffed the notes under her seat.

'Sorry. Sometimes it's very difficult. You'll understand later when I tell you.'

Margaret placed the hot fish pie on the table and poured herself a glass of wine. She seemed very relaxed and drank almost the whole glass in one go.

'As soon as we've finished supper we'll talk about the future. You're the only person who will ever know. I need you, Barbara.'

Barbara ate hungrily. The fish pie was delicious. But at the same time she couldn't wait for the table to be cleared so that Margaret would talk.

It was so frustrating. Margaret insisted that they wash the dishes and stoke the fire first. She fetched a bottle of brandy and poured a glass for each of them. Then she opened the drawer where she had put the Bible and brought it to the table.

'Sit down, Barbara.' She gestured for Barbara to sit at the table and then locked the door, pocketing the key. 'I don't think we'll be disturbed, but just in case.'

Barbara was surer than ever that there was someone living upstairs.

Margaret sat in the big armchair close to the blazing fire. She looked very composed, with her hands folded in her lap. She was silent for a while, but then she started to talk.

'When my husband was killed I just wanted to die ... to die and be buried beside him. Suddenly my life was in pieces. I had always longed to have Armande's child and now that would never happen. Can you imagine how I felt?'

Barbara shook her head. There was no need to say anything.

'When Armande died, Julia took charge. My sister was such a strong woman. She was always the dominant one. Even though all I wanted was to be alone, she insisted that I should continue working.'

Margaret described how terrible it had been even to contemplate a return to acting. She constantly broke down in tears. Eventually the producers agreed that she should take a few months off.

'I couldn't stand to be in our little house with its memories. We'd bought it together. It was just close to Ladbroke Grove. I knew I was losing control. I didn't want to get out of bed. In fact, I didn't want to do anything and Julia became very worried about me.'

Margaret stared into the fire.

'I overdosed on sleeping tablets. Julia called an ambulance and I was taken into hospital. I hardly knew where I was. She was very protective, as the press were constantly outside. I became very unstable . . .'

Barbara stifled a yawn. Most of what Margaret was saying she already knew. She couldn't wait for her to get to the 'secret'.

It took quite a long time. Margaret explained how she'd been taken into a clinic in a blur. Eventually Julia had collected her and driven her back to the manor house. She was there for Emily's second birthday. Emily was Julia's beloved daughter. For the first time since Armande's death, Margaret began to feel better. She described the adorable little girl and how just being with Emily made her realize that life without Armande was possible.

Barbara impatiently sipped her brandy.

'My sister's betrayal was so deep. I'd had no idea she could be so devious. I trusted him. I adored him. If I had known about it when he was alive, I don't know what I'd have done.'

Barbara leaned forward, wondering if she'd missed something.

'I don't understand. Did you say "betrayal"?'

Margaret nodded. She said that Julia had never married and never admitted who the little girl's father was. Julia had simply told her it was a relationship that didn't work out. It had never occurred to Margaret that she knew him.

Shortly after Margaret married Armande, Julia sold her mews cottage in London. She'd subsequently bought the manor house to refurbish it and make some money. Armande had helped Julia move and spent a lot of time with her at the manor. Margaret had been working on the television series then. She was wondrously happy, married to a man she adored and enjoying huge success with the show. She never suspected for a second that Armande and Julia were having an affair.

Barbara began to understand. This was really shocking and she knew it would make big tabloid news. She poured herself another brandy.

'My goodness, when did you find out?'

Margaret gave a long, shuddering sigh. She leaned back and closed her eyes.

'After Armande died I continued working in London. I had by now sold my house and moved closer to the studios. It was about this time of year and I would often come out here for weekends. The weekend it happened, I decided not to drive down as it was snowing. Instead I invited Julia and Emily up to London.'

Margaret rose and sat opposite Barbara at the table. She drew the Bible close to her and turned to the first page, where her sister's name was written. Beside the name was a dark brown stain.

'This is Julia's blood,' she whispered. 'Now I want you to lay your hand over the cross.'

When Barbara did so, she could feel it beneath her palm.

'You must swear never to repeat what I'm going to tell you.'

'Yes, I do. I do.'

'No, I want you to say it.'

Barbara didn't give a toss about swearing on the Bible. She was not remotely religious and hadn't been to church since she was a child. But as she waited for Margaret's instructions, the handle on the kitchen door rattled. Then it turned, as if someone was trying to get in.

Margaret sprang up.

'Stay here. Let me sort this out. She's being very naughty. Please don't do anything until I get back.'

Barbara couldn't believe it. Just as it seemed they were getting somewhere! She wondered if it was Julia who was locked in upstairs. But what about the classroom? Maybe it was Emily.

She frowned, trying to think of what Alan had said. He'd told her that shortly after Armande died in the helicopter crash, Margaret suffered another terrible tragedy. What was that?

Barbara sat back. She'd always had a very vivid imagination and now it ran riot. What if none of it were true? What if Armande was upstairs? Perhaps he'd survived the helicopter crash and was badly burned. Or what if he'd suffered terrible head injuries and lost his mind?

She felt almost feverish. Could it be that, after she discovered their betrayal, Margaret had locked Armande or Julia away? Or maybe punished their child instead?

Shaking, she gulped down her brandy. She

heard a door closing above. Then the soft footfall of someone hurrying down the stairs.

Barbara's heart was beating fast and her hands were clenched tightly together as the kitchen door creaked open.

Chapter Nine

Margaret stood in the doorway, smiling.

'It's all quiet now,' she said. 'Are you all right, Barbara? You look very agitated.'

'I'm fine. It's . . . it's just the fire. It makes the room very warm,' Barbara stammered.

Margaret leaned over and touched Barbara's face.

'You're so flushed. Would you like me to make you a coffee?'

'No, really. We were interrupted and you were just about to ask me something.'

'You've had too much to drink,' Margaret teased.

'Look, I'm ready.' Barbara pressed her hand on top of the Bible. 'Just tell me what you want me to say.'

Margaret nodded and closed her eyes, placing her hands together as if in prayer.

'Repeat these words: "I promise that I will never divulge this secret to anyone. It must remain with me and my knowing will release Margaret from all her promised responsibilities. This I swear."'

When Barbara had said the words, Margaret touched her hand.

'Thank you.'

Although Barbara now did feel a little woozy, she was desperate for Margaret to continue. Impatiently, she asked, 'Who is upstairs? I know someone is living up there.'

Margaret sipped her glass of brandy.

Then, not looking at Barbara, she resumed her story. She repeated that she'd arranged for Julia and Emily to stay with her in London. It was snowing. The roads were icy. When Julia had not arrived by eleven, she became worried. At midnight she received a call from St Mary's Hospital in Paddington. There had been an accident and her sister was in intensive care. She rang for a taxi and went straight to the hospital.

Julia was in a critical condition, desperate to talk to Margaret. Margaret screamed at the doctors to give her a few moments alone with her sister. At that point, Julia had clung to Margaret's hand and admitted that Emily was Armande's child. She said that the affair was over as quickly as it had begun. She wept and asked to be forgiven.

Margaret shuddered and sipped more brandy.

'I was in shock, hardly able to take in what she was saying. I didn't want to believe it.'

Julia then became hysterical, asking Margaret to go to her bag and bring her the Bible from inside it. Julia insisted that Margaret put her hand over the cross and swear on her life that she would take care of Emily. If anything should happen to Julia, Margaret must swear to bring up Emily as her own child.

'Of course I did as she asked. And that seemed to calm her. When the doctors returned she had become quieter. But then she suddenly went into convulsions. Blood poured from her nose and mouth ... it was terrible. She'd been bleeding in her brain and had sunk into a coma shortly afterwards. She had been dying in front of me all the time.'

Barbara now knew how the blood had stained the Bible. She wanted to reach out to comfort Margaret, but there seemed to be no need. Margaret was in a world of her own. She sat very still, calmly sipping her brandy.

'So Emily was injured as well?' Barbara asked.

Margaret nodded. She explained that she had been in a state of shock over her sister's confession, hardly able to take in that she had died. Eventually she'd asked if she could see Emily.

'I was told she'd been taken straight to Great

Ormond Street, so I caught another taxi and went straight there.'

Even though Margaret's story was so shocking, Barbara couldn't contain her excitement any longer. 'She's here, isn't she? It's Emily I've heard moving around upstairs, isn't it?'

Margaret nodded.

'When I got to the hospital, they told me that Emily was dead on arrival. I broke down in tears. To lose my husband, then my sister, then her child ... It was all too much for me. I collapsed and the following day I was taken back to the clinic to recover. Do you understand what I'm telling you?'

Puzzled, Barbara frowned and shook her head. She had no idea how to react when Margaret continued, explaining that she'd managed to leave the clinic and go to the funerals. She then came straight to the manor house.

Margaret paused and looked straight at Barbara. With no emotion in her voice, she stated, 'That's when I realized Emily had returned.'

Barbara could think of nothing to say.

'She lives here, Barbara. She's now seven years old. I've taken care of her all this time. I've been afraid to tell anyone. I knew no one would believe me. They'd send me back to that awful clinic. Emily has dominated my life. I've treated her like the daughter I never had. I couldn't just leave her and return to work. That was impossible.'

Barbara's jaw dropped. She tried to say something, but no words came out. She was certain that Margaret was mentally ill. She didn't want to upset her any further. She just wanted to leave and get back to London as soon as possible. She knew about how schizophrenics could hear or speak in different voices. Eventually she found her own voice.

'Thank you for telling me this, Margaret. I will never repeat it to anyone.'

Margaret gave her a lovely smile.

'Of course you won't. I knew I could trust you. Now we share the secret, I'm so relieved that it's over.'

Margaret woke Barbara at seven the following morning. She was very smartly dressed. Her face was made up and her hair was coiled into a bun at the base of her neck.

'I've run a bath for you. We'll leave in about three-quarters of an hour.'

'Terrific,' Barbara muttered, feeling the start of a terrible hangover.

She went upstairs, where Margaret had left

out clean underwear and a lovely skirt with a thick cashmere sweater. She then came back down to the kitchen and made a cup of coffee.

The drive to the station passed without incident. Margaret kept up a bubbly conversation, pointing out the landmarks in the village. First the church and the vicarage, then the neat little cottages and some elegant weekend retreats for people from London, finally the post office and the grocer's shop.

When they stopped in the small railway station car park, she showed Barbara where she hid the keys of the Land Rover, beneath the driver's seat.

They were in perfect time for the train and sat opposite each other in window seats. Margaret said she would take a taxi from Waterloo to her solicitor in Knightsbridge. Barbara said she would head over to Alan and Kevin's house. She had still not made contact, as her mobile phone battery was now flat.

As they arrived, Barbara was a little embarrassed to admit that she had only a few pound coins. Margaret gave her two £20 and three £5 notes.

'That's too much.'

'Nonsense. You will need to buy a few things.'

Margaret put her briefcase down and cupped Barbara's face in her hands. She kissed her on the lips.

'Goodbye, Barbara. I love you.'

Barbara was embarrassed again, but replied haltingly, 'Er, I love you too, Margaret.'

Sitting back in a taxi, Barbara felt very confused. Her headache was really hammering. She lowered the window and took a few deep breaths. She began to wonder if she could still face speaking to Mike Phillips, the editor, about all this. It was so crazy, how would he react?

As she paid the taxi fare, Barbara hoped that someone would be at home, because she didn't have her spare key. She rang the doorbell and waited. Thankfully, Kevin was in.

He was very different in appearance from Alan. He was squat, with thick dark hair worn in a crew cut. His broad shoulders looked even broader in the thick plaid dressing gown he was now wearing. He didn't look very welcoming. In fact, he asked straight away when she would be leaving, reminding her that he needed to use the box room.

Barbara promised him that she was going to look at some places to rent, but it didn't seem to make him any friendlier. He told her to help herself to coffee, then went back upstairs.

Barbara took a cup of tepid coffee up to the box room to recharge her mobile. Sitting on the bed, she felt like crying.

She opened her laptop to check her emails. There weren't any. She took out of her handbag the scrawled notes she had made while at the manor house and began to copy them into a document, recalling the strange way Margaret had behaved.

The telephone rang and she heard someone hurrying to answer it. Then, after a moment, Kevin knocked on her door.

'There's a Mr Sullivan on the line for you. Can you take it downstairs? He wouldn't tell me what he wanted.'

Barbara closed her laptop, went to the kitchen and picked up the receiver.

'Hello?'

'Am I speaking to Miss Barbara Hardy?'

'Yes.'

'My name is Edward Sullivan. I am Margaret Reynolds's solicitor.'

Barbara could hardly take in what he had said. In a very abrupt tone of voice, he informed her he needed to see her as soon as possible. She would have to sign various important documents. When Barbara asked what these were, he replied that he did not wish to discuss it over the telephone.

As she'd nothing better to do, she agreed to meet him at his Knightsbridge office. They made an appointment for three fifteen.

Barbara peeked into the kitchen as she was leaving.

'I'm off now. I'll be back later if that's all right?'

Kevin was scrambling some eggs.

'Yeah, it's fine. Alan should be home.'

He hesitated, then said, 'By the way, that job you offered me. My agent hasn't got any booking.'

Barbara tried to think quickly, which was hard with her hangover. Finally, she said, 'Well, my editor still has to finalize stuff. I think we're supposed to have a meeting this afternoon.'

She was just closing the door when he asked, 'It isn't connected to Margaret Reynolds, is it?'

Barbara pretended not to hear him and didn't reply.

Kevin had just sat down to eat when he heard Barbara's mobile phone ringing from the box room. She must have forgotten to take it off charge. He picked it up just as it stopped ringing. The caller ID showed 'Mike Phillips, editor'.

Kevin couldn't resist it. He pressed redial and waited. Mike answered.

'Hi, I'm a friend of Barbara's. Can I take a message?'

'I've been waiting for her to get back to me about some mad ageing soap star,' Mike said sharply. 'Barbara was supposed to track her down for a feature.'

'Mad . . . ageing . . .' Kevin repeated.

'Yeah. She said she might be returning to work.'

'I see,' Kevin said quietly. He promised Mike that he would pass on the message.

His scrambled eggs had gone cold, but he was too furious to eat. Instead he called Alan.

'She's going to expose Margaret. I'm damn sure that was her intention all along. Persuading you to take her to the party so she could get the dirt on the poor woman.'

'I don't believe it!' Alan said.

'You'd better, because I talked to her editor. I warned you. She's poison. When you get back tonight, we'll deal with her.'

'I should be home about five.'

Kevin stormed outside to the small courtyard and lit a cigarette. He'd been trying to give up smoking because Alan loathed it, but he was so angry now he couldn't help himself.

When he had finished his cigarette, he went to the box room, picked up Barbara's suitcases and laptop, and took them down to the hall.

Barbara caught the tube to Knightsbridge and walked from there to Mr Sullivan's office, which was on the ground floor of an elegant house. She rang the doorbell and a secretary led her into a small waiting room.

After five minutes, Edward Sullivan walked in. He was very tall and thin-faced, with a shock of thick white hair. He wore a smart navy-blue pinstriped suit.

'You must be Barbara Hardy,' he said, shaking her hand. 'Please come into my office.'

The room was dominated by a large oak desk with claw feet. A computer and telephone were to one side. On a large leather-backed blotter were numerous documents clipped together.

'What is this about?' Barbara said nervously.

He gave her a quizzical glance.

'You have been named as the legal heir to Miss Reynolds's estate.'

'I don't understand.'

Sullivan proceeded to explain that she was to

inherit the manor house and a substantial sum of money. The conditions of the inheritance were rather irregular. She was to agree to live at the manor house and to keep the promise she had made while she was a recent guest there.

'Do you recall making Miss Reynolds a promise to shoulder her responsibilities?'

'Well, yes, I do. But I am not sure of the exact details.'

Barbara started to panic. She was hardly able to draw breath.

'This is obviously in the event of Miss Reynolds's death,' Sullivan said.

Barbara shook her head, completely baffled.

The main condition was that Barbara must sign a legally binding document agreeing to live at the manor house. If she refused, or left after a short period, the will would become null and void.

Mr Sullivan also confirmed what Margaret had told her about planning permission. But apparently the will stipulated that no part of the manor house could be sold or divided into apartments.

Barbara was still confused, but agreed to sign all the documents. After doing so, she asked why Margaret had made her the heir. 'Is she all right?'

'She seemed in very good spirits when she came here this morning. Why do you ask?'

'I mean is she what they call "of sound mind"?'

He gave a shrug as he carefully stacked all the papers.

'She certainly seemed very alert and positive earlier. I am aware she's had some problems in the past, but not for some time. I will need contact details from you, Miss Hardy, as I will send copies of everything.'

Barbara gave him Alan and Kevin's address and telephone number, as well as her mobile number.

She headed back to the tube station in a daze. Nothing made sense to her. She couldn't understand why Margaret had done this. Then, remembering the kiss, she decided not to think about it any more.

Chapter Ten

'You won't believe what just happened this afternoon,' Barbara said when Kevin opened the front door.

He picked up one of her cases.

'I've got a damned good idea. You're not welcome here, Barbara, so take your cases and get out.'

'But just let me tell you.'

Kevin hurled a case out on to the front step.

'Let me tell you something. I talked to your editor. You don't have a commission! You lied to me! You lied to Alan! I won't have anything to do with your seedy, nasty attempt at writing about Margaret. She's had enough of the press.'

Alan had joined Kevin by now. He chipped in that he blamed himself for being so naive.

The second case was hurled out, then Kevin shoved Barbara's laptop into her arms and slammed the door shut.

Barbara burst into tears and rang the bell again, keeping her finger on it until Alan opened the door.

'I left my mobile on charge.'

Alan and Kevin waited in silence as she marched upstairs and down again, stuffing her phone and charger into her pocket.

She turned a sullen face towards Kevin.

'There are other photographers. I was only doing you a favour.'

The door slammed shut a second time. With little choice, Barbara stumbled off down the road with her heavy cases. After a while, she stopped and took out her mobile to ring Margaret. There was no reply, so she picked up her cases again. There was nowhere else for her to go but back to the manor house. She was confident of a welcome, especially after learning about Margaret's will.

It was eight that evening when Alan received a call from Edward Sullivan, who sounded anxious. He said that he needed to speak to Miss Hardy urgently concerning the whereabouts of Miss Reynolds.

Alan replied that he only had the address and phone number for the manor house.

'I have called the landline and Miss Hardy's

mobile phone numerous times, but there is no answer.'

Alan said he was sorry but could not help any further.

Meanwhile, Barbara was on the train heading back to the manor house. She had tried to call ahead when she got on the train, but there was no reply. After that, she turned her mobile off.

At the station Margaret's Land Rover was parked, unlocked, where she'd left it. Barbara felt beneath the driver's seat for the keys. She didn't question why Margaret had made sure that she knew where they could be found. She was just grateful that the engine turned over.

Barbara drove carefully, as it was dark by now. She recalled Margaret giving her details of the route as they had driven to the station. The church and vicarage were in darkness as she went by on her way to the narrow, bumpy lane.

She had to get out and heave open the white wooden gate that blocked her path. She then continued up the winding drive until she reached the old manor house that waited, dark and foreboding. She fumbled with various keys before she found the one that opened the heavy front door. It was not until she was in the dark hallway that she began to feel uneasy. When she attempted to switch on the lights, there was an ominous click. Nothing. The house felt very cold and very obviously empty.

Without a fire, the kitchen was colder than she remembered. Only the Aga was warm. Barbara found the firelighters and made a fire in the grate. It caught quickly and lit up the room. Next she found some candles. As soon as the room began to warm up, she felt less afraid. In the flickering candlelight, she fetched her suitcases.

She found a tin of tomato soup in the pantry and emptied it into a pan. She then cut two thick slices of bread and lifted up the Aga's hot plate to make lovely crisp toast.

Barbara ate hungrily, and after the thick buttered toast and tomato soup she began to feel more relaxed. She even opened one of the screw-top wine bottles in the rack.

She moved closer to the fire and sipped her third glass of wine. It was almost ten o'clock and still no word from Margaret. She wondered if she should call Alan to see if they had heard from her, but decided against it. As they'd thrown her out, it probably wasn't advisable.

It was the silence that she found disconcerting. No noise from the water pipes or the old central-heating system. It was very, very quiet.

She tried the light switch again, but still nothing happened. She turned on the radio but couldn't find any programme without static. She checked the batteries, but if they needed to be replaced she hadn't the slightest idea where the new ones would be.

Then she remembered the notebook that Margaret had left. Even with the light from the fire and the candles, it was very difficult to read the scrawled lists. Barbara licked her thumb, turning page after page. By holding a candle closer, she was able to make out instructions for checking the generator in the basement. But she didn't know where that was. She wondered if someone had simply turned off the electricity. It seemed to be as temperamental as Margaret had said.

There was no way she was going to look for the basement tonight. It was scary enough being alone in the warm kitchen. But she did need to use the lavatory.

Holding a candlestick aloft, she headed for the downstairs bathroom. It was inky black in the hallway. The sounds of the old house creaking and groaning unnerved her. Outside the wind blew eerily, rattling the windows.

She had just reached the bathroom when she heard the telephone ring. The sound made her literally jump. She pulled the old lavatory chain and snatched the candlestick, causing the flame to flicker and die. She swore. The loud ringing of the telephone continued as she headed slowly back down the hallway. It was so dark that she had to feel her way along the wall. The light shone beneath the door but it seemed to take for ever to reach the kitchen.

She sighed with relief as she made it. But just as her hand reached out for the receiver the phone stopped ringing.

'Hello? Hello?'

Barbara tried to remember what to dial to check the caller but couldn't, so she hung up.

She was certain it had to be Margaret. Was she at the station, waiting to be collected? Barbara checked the book hanging on the old piece of string. The train station was listed, but there was no reply when she rang. By now it was after eleven, so she tried the taxi service. If Margaret had arrived and found the Land Rover missing, perhaps she was getting a cab home.

'Hello. I'm calling to see if Miss Reynolds has booked a taxi for this evening.'

A sleepy voice said that she hadn't.

'Do you know if there are any trains due?'

'No, miss. The last train came in at nine.'

Barbara put more logs on the fire and then noticed the blanket she'd used the previous night. It was folded over the arm of the big Chesterfield. Beneath was the white nightdress, also neatly folded. It was as if Margaret had expected Barbara would be staying another night.

She wrapped herself in the blanket and lay down on the sofa. At one point she was sure that she heard someone knocking at the window. She made herself get up and check, but it was a branch tapping against the glass. She locked the kitchen door and lay down again.

Eventually, she was forced to pull the blanket over her head, because another sound was making her tremble. She couldn't really make it out. Was it a child crying or the wind outside? Finally, she fell asleep.

And because she was asleep, Barbara didn't hear the sound of continuous weeping. Didn't hear the footsteps. Didn't hear or see the handle of the kitchen door turning.

Chapter Eleven

Barbara was woken by the shrill ringing of the telephone. Disorientated, she got up, almost tripping over the blanket.

'Hello?'

'Barbara?' It was Alan. 'Have you had the news on?'

'I've only just woken up. What time is it?'

'You don't know, then.'

'Know what?'

'It's been on the television.'

'I don't know what you're talking about.'

'It's Margaret.'

'She's not here. I expected her home last night, but she never turned up,' Barbara began defensively, but something in Alan's tone made her ask, 'Has something happened to her?'

Sounding very upset, Alan told her that Margaret had thrown herself in front of a tube train at seven thirty the previous evening.

'Oh, my God! That's terrible.'

Barbara slid down the wall to sit on the floor.

'Was it an accident?' she gasped.

'According to the TV news, she was standing very close to the edge of the platform.'

'I can't take this in,' Barbara said, close to tears.

'A Mr Sullivan called twice, wanting to speak to you. As I had no idea where you were, I said I'd ring around to try and give you the news.'

'Thank you.' Her voice was hardly audible.

'He wants to see you urgently, so you'd better ring him.'

'Yes, of course. I will.'

After a long pause, Alan hung up. Barbara was certain he'd wanted to say more but was too upset.

She staggered to her feet and replaced the receiver. She was in such a state of shock that she wasn't sure what to do. After searching in the pantry, she found a half-bottle of Scotch and poured herself a stiff drink.

When the phone rang yet again, it made her jump with nerves.

This time it was Mr Sullivan, requesting in a brusque tone that she come to see him as soon as possible. He said he was certain she knew what it was about. He hung up before she had time to question him further.

Barbara drained her glass of Scotch before

driving to the station. There she sat in the freezing-cold waiting room until the next train to London left.

It wasn't until she took her seat on the train that she thought about her initial meeting with the solicitor. She stared out of the window in horror as she realized that Margaret must have intended not to return to the manor house. Why else had she gone to such lengths to alter her will?

It was only now that Barbara digested the fact that she was to inherit the manor house.

Barbara took a taxi straight to Knightsbridge and Edward Sullivan ushered her into his office.

'This is obviously a sad time. I am very distressed, especially having spent so long with Margaret yesterday morning. She gave me no indication of her intentions. Shocking, so shocking.'

'Yes,' Barbara said, her head bowed.

Mr Sullivan took out a white handkerchief and blew his nose loudly.

'There will be an inquest, of course. I was questioned by the police.'

Barbara nodded.

'They wanted to know when I'd last seen

her. I had to confirm that Margaret had arranged yesterday's meeting. I stressed that she displayed no emotional problems. To the contrary, she appeared very calm. In fact, she was very positive and clear about her intentions. Of course, I had to tell them about her changing her will.'

Barbara nodded again.

'I also gave them your name as the main beneficiary.'

He hesitated, twisting a pen in his long bony fingers.

'I will require some more signatures, Miss Hardy. Obviously, until the coroner's report nothing can be forwarded to you with regard to your inheritance.'

Barbara was in a daze as she signed the papers. When he asked for her contact details, she didn't know what to say.

'Well, I was at the manor house last night.'

'Until all this is sorted, perhaps you shouldn't return ... although I'm sure Margaret's intentions were for you to live there on a permanent basis. We did read through her conditions for you to inherit, didn't we?'

He looked at Barbara, who was so stupefied he asked if she needed a glass of water. She shook her head.

'You signed the papers to say that you agreed to all her requests, yes?'

Barbara nodded, but her mind was a total blank. And when she left the office shortly afterwards she was at a loss where to go.

Part of her wanted to call Alan and Kevin, but she couldn't stand the thought of being rejected. Instead, she decided to take a bus to their house. Gazing out of the window, she couldn't help but notice newspaper stands displaying the terrible headlines:

'Famous TV Star Jumps to Death'
'Tragic Star's Suicide'
'TV Star's Tragic Death'

By the time she rang Alan and Kevin's doorbell she was crying for the first time since she'd been told about Margaret.

When Alan opened the door, she was sobbing.

'Oh, Alan, please let me in. I've got nowhere else to go.'

Alan put his arm around her shoulders.

'It's all right. You can stay here.'

Kevin emerged from their kitchen as Alan closed the front door. He gave the distressed Barbara a cold look.

'They're showing all the old clips from the show on the news reports. I hope for your sake you didn't have anything to do with her suicide.'

Chapter Twelve

Barbara unpacked the few things she'd brought with her and lay down on the single bed. She'd made no mention of the will. There had been no opportunity as they sat watching the television news about Margaret. Alan had become very distressed and had broken down in tears.

At six o'clock she heard the doorbell ring. Shortly after, Alan knocked on the box-room door.

'There are two police officers downstairs. They want to talk to you.'

Detective Inspector John Douglas introduced himself as Barbara entered the kitchen. A female detective, Angela Collins, was with him. She shook Barbara's hand and they took their seats at the kitchen table. Alan and Kevin hovered and Barbara wished they would leave them in private.

She told the detectives everything she could about Margaret.

'So you went back to the manor house yesterday evening?' asked Douglas.

'Yes. I just said so.'

'Did anyone see you arrive?'

'I suppose the ticket collector might remember seeing me.'

There was a pause and then Detective Inspector Douglas nodded to his companion, who continued.

'So Miss Reynolds gave you permission to return there, did she?'

Barbara hesitated and then nodded. Alan glanced at Kevin, knowing this was not exactly true, as she'd tried to stay with them.

The female detective asked how Barbara thought Miss Reynolds appeared. 'Did she seem distressed? Nervous? Show any signs that she intended to kill herself?'

'No, she was very relaxed. She said she would be seeing her solicitor.'

Now Detective Inspector Douglas resumed. They knew from Mr Sullivan that she'd gone to his office that afternoon. Barbara nodded, glancing at Alan and Kevin.

'Yes, I kept the appointment at three fifteen.'

'Did you see Miss Reynolds after that meeting?'

'No. I came here and then caught the seven fifteen train.'

'So you never saw her again?'

'No, I didn't.'

'You're sure about that?'

'Yes, I'm sure. In fact, I went there because I presumed that she'd returned home.'

'She didn't call you or try to get in touch with you?'

'No.'

Detective Inspector Douglas then dropped his bombshell.

'You see, Miss Hardy, we have to make certain that it was a tragic accident, or suicide, rather than murder.'

Barbara turned to Alan and back to the detectives.

'I don't understand. From the news, it seems she committed suicide. She jumped in front of the tube train, didn't she?'

Neither detective replied. Instead, they studied their notebooks.

'Was it not an accident, then?' Barbara asked.

Without replying to her question, Detective Inspector Douglas asked Barbara if she had found a letter of any kind at the manor house. Barbara answered that she had not.

'So, Miss Hardy, when Miss Reynolds was at the tube station in London, you were heading for the manor house?'

'Yes.'

'You were not at the tube station?'

'No. I've already told you I was on the train.'

Detective Inspector Douglas snapped his notebook closed, as if the interview was over. But it wasn't.

'You see, we have to question anyone who might benefit from Miss Reynolds's death.'

Alan and Kevin looked confused.

'And you are Miss Reynolds's main beneficiary.'

Alan's jaw dropped.

'What? She couldn't be! She hardly knew her!'

'Nevertheless, yesterday morning Miss Reynolds altered her will to name Miss Hardy as her heir. That same afternoon, Miss Hardy, you met with Mr Sullivan, who told you about the will. Isn't that right?'

Shaking, Barbara nodded.

'Yes. But I had no idea of her intentions. She'd said nothing to me.'

Kevin stared at the detectives.

'Is this true? Did Margaret really change her will the same day that she died?'

Detective Inspector Douglas nodded, keeping his eyes on Barbara.

'We have a witness who was standing not far from Miss Reynolds at the tube station. She claims that Miss Reynolds was waiting very close to the edge of the platform. It looked to her, from the way that Miss Reynolds jerked forward on to the line just as the train arrived, as if someone pushed her.'

'Did this witness see someone behind Margaret?' demanded Kevin.

'That's unclear. The platform wasn't crowded and it appears that no one was standing close to her,' Detective Inspector Douglas said.

'Then why does she say Margaret was pushed?' Alan asked.

Apparently the witness thought Margaret was pushed in the small of her back and fell forward, unable to stop herself. They were waiting for CCTV footage to see if there was anything to confirm this.

The detectives thanked Barbara for her cooperation and asked if she would be staying with her friends in case they wished to talk to her again.

Barbara glanced at Alan and Kevin, saying that if she wasn't at this address she could be contacted on her mobile.

As soon as the detectives left, Kevin confronted Barbara.

'You really are a piece of work.'

He sat in the same chair Detective Inspector Douglas had used.

'Right, Barbara, start talking, and the truth this time. Why did Margaret make you her beneficiary so shortly after meeting you?'

Barbara shook her head, saying it was exactly as she'd told the detectives.

'She never talked to you about it?' Alan asked.

'No. And to be honest, I thought she was behaving strangely the night before. But when we got on the train she seemed fine. It never occurred to me that she was even thinking about suicide.'

She started to cry and Kevin leaned across the table in barely controlled fury.

'Bit late for tears, isn't it? Just what did you do?'

Barbara wiped her cheeks with the back of her hand. She swore she hadn't known about the will until she met Sullivan.

'I couldn't make it out. He asked me to sign all these papers. I even told him that it was ridiculous.'

'You must have done something,' Alan insisted.

Barbara hesitated, then took a deep breath.

'If you must know, the previous night I really did think she was unbalanced.'

Kevin and Alan waited. Gradually Barbara told them about the time she'd spent at the manor house. She explained that she was certain someone else was living there, that Margaret constantly talked to someone but she'd never seen them.

'She would lock me in the kitchen. I would hear her talking and playing the piano upstairs. It was really starting to freak me out. I wondered if her husband had survived the helicopter crash or if it was her sister, or her sister's little girl. I was really scared . . . and the lights kept going off.'

'You've got a vivid imagination,' Kevin said, shaking his head in disgust.

'I really thought she needed to see a shrink. She brought out this awful Bible, asking me to swear on it that I would never tell anyone what she was going to tell me.'

'Go on,' Kevin said.

'It was mad . . . something about taking care of her sister's child. But then she told me the girl was dead. She said she was scared to tell anyone because she thought they'd put her back into some mental institution.'

She paused.

'There's also something else.'

Barbara felt extremely uneasy repeating it, thinking that it might have been the trigger that made Margaret jump in front of the tube.

'She told me her sister had admitted as she was dying that she and Armande had been lovers.'

'I don't believe that for a second,' Alan said furiously, and began pacing around the kitchen. 'I've never seen two people more in love. He wouldn't have betrayed Margaret, and especially not with her sister. It's all lies.'

Barbara became angry.

'I'm only telling you what Margaret told me.'

Alan banged the table with his hand.

'You're making this up! You just want to get that article written now that Margaret is dead and can't sue.'

'I'm not making it up,' Barbara cried.

Kevin jumped up now and the pair of them faced Barbara.

'If you dare print a word of this . . .'

Now Barbara stood up too in a fury.

'I'm not writing it. That's the truth.'

Alan gave her a look of such disapproval that she felt like bursting into tears again.

'You know what I think? As Margaret's heir, you won't need to write tripe for anyone ever again, because she must have left a fortune.'

Kevin joined in.

'I think you blackmailed her into changing her will.'

'I DID NOT,' Barbara shouted back.

'When the police asked you how Margaret was, you said she was relaxed and happy. Now you tell us she was unbalanced. Why didn't you say that to the police?'

Barbara clenched her hands into fists.

'Because I told them the truth. She did seem fine and happy, as if a weight had been lifted from her shoulders.'

Kevin leaned very close, his voice quiet and threatening.

'You had a big motive to push her in front of the tube. I hope you were telling the truth, Barbara. If they find out that you not only lied about Margaret's state of mind but were also somewhere near when she fell—'

'I was on the train going to the manor house!'

'Then for your sake I hope they're able to prove it.'

Chapter Thirteen

Barbara had nowhere else to stay but at Alan and Kevin's, even though they didn't want her there. She did make a half-hearted attempt to find somewhere else, but she felt so depressed she couldn't face getting out of bed. They virtually ignored her, behaving as if she wasn't there.

Detective Inspector Douglas got in touch to inform her that the CCTV footage had shown no one close to Margaret, even if it did seem as if she was pushed forward. They had therefore decided that Margaret committed suicide.

Alan was contacted by Mr Sullivan to discuss the funeral arrangements. He was taken aback to learn that Margaret had left precise instructions about what was to happen in the event of her death. She had made a list of the close friends she wanted to be at the service and she asked to be buried beside her husband. She had left a considerable sum of money to cover the costs.

As soon as Alan heard this, he realized that

Margaret had planned everything. Tragically, she really had intended to kill herself.

He got in touch with the cast of *Harwood House* and told them about the funeral. Barbara's name was not included on the list. Both Alan and Kevin still believed that she had tipped Margaret over the edge, if not the edge of the station platform, then of her sanity.

Barbara had asked Mr Sullivan if he could release some of the money left to her, but he had told her coldly that it would take time.

So, without funds, Barbara really had no option but to remain in Kingston, with Alan and Kevin.

The day of the funeral was overcast. Barbara stayed in the box room, seething with anger. She decided that she would do as requested and not go to the service. However, she did wonder about going to the grave. She might do that, even if it meant standing some distance away from everyone else.

Kevin knocked on her door and came in to tell her that they were leaving. She shrugged. He didn't bother to ask if she was all right. She turned away from him, frowning in agitation.

'I won't be here when you get back.'

He raised his eyebrows.

'I'll go to the manor house, seeing as it's rightfully mine now. Besides, it's obvious I'm not welcome here.'

'Whatever you want. It has always been that way with you anyway.'

He closed the door behind him and joined Alan downstairs.

'It's all right. She's not coming.'

Alan hesitated.

'Did you tell her?'

'No. Why should I? It's got nothing to do with her.'

Barbara watched them leave. Then, turning away from the window, she began to pack her suitcase. She was checking to make sure she'd left nothing behind when the telephone rang. By the time she picked up the receiver it had gone on to voicemail.

It felt odd to hear the sound of Mike Phillips's voice again.

'Kevin, just wondering how soon you'll be able to get the funeral pictures to me. Plenty of shots of the actors at the graveside, yes? And tell Alan I'll need his article as soon as possible. I want lots of stuff about his time working with Margaret.'

'You two-faced bastard,' Barbara hissed.

114

The call made up her mind: she would definitely go to the cemetery.

Beside Margaret's open grave, next to the one holding her beloved Armande, was the headstone for her sister, Julia. There were fresh white lilies in an ornate vase there, but on the stone there was no mention of her young daughter.

Barbara took up her position, hiding behind a large marble angel. Margaret's funeral procession was heading through the cemetery gates. The hearse was covered in hundreds of lilies.

She watched all the actors following the hearse. She could see Kevin turn to wag his finger at a number of photographers. As he headed back to the others, he had to pass within feet of Barbara.

He was shocked when she dived out from behind the angel.

'I know what you're doing. You disgust me. All the fuss about me writing about Margaret and you're doing it yourself.'

He took hold of her arm.

'Let go of me,' she shouted.

Everyone turned as Kevin pushed her away. She stumbled and fell, bursting into tears. She remained curled up on the ground.

As the coffin was slowly lowered into the grave, the minister began to read from his Bible.

People threw furtive glances towards Barbara as she got to her feet, dusting down her skirt. Then it happened.

At first Barbara was unsure. Maybe she had touched the cold marble angel. But that was some distance away. Then she felt it, a small icy-cold hand holding hers. She tried to shake it away.

'Can we go home now?'

The voice was high-pitched, like a child's. She felt the tiny cold hand grip tightly, pulling her forward. Barbara's heart began to pound in her chest.

'Go away,' she said, trying to release her hand.

'No, I won't. You promised to take care of me.'

Barbara wondered if she was going mad. This couldn't be happening.

The little voice continued, 'Your suitcase. Pick up your suitcase.'

Barbara snatched it up and the child broke free. She saw her then. It was Emily, the little girl in the photograph at the manor house.

Barbara glanced towards the mourners.

Could they see the child? But they were all turned towards the grave as the minister closed his Bible.

'Ashes to ashes. Dust to dust.'

No sooner than the image of Emily materialized, it faded. Barbara ran from the cemetery. Her heart was still pounding as she hurried past the gathered reporters.

Felicity watched Barbara's hasty exit and said quietly to Alan, 'I've just had a really strange flashback. Real déjà vu.'

'What do you mean?'

'I was here with Margaret when she buried her sister and something very peculiar happened. Margaret was standing next to me and suddenly she was really freaked out. I wasn't sure what to do. She started talking loudly and behaving oddly. Then she turned and ran away.'

'Well, it's understandable. First her husband and then her sister, and wasn't her young niece also killed in the accident?'

'Yes, but she never came back for drinks at my house. I'd arranged for everyone to be there. She returned to the manor house and I didn't really see her again until we all went there last month.'

Felicity held on to Alan's arm.

'It's funny. She never put the little one's name on her sister's grave. Emily, I think it was.'

Alan was not really listening to her any longer. He was eager to keep up as people began to leave.

'The way Barbara behaved just then, shaking her hand. That was exactly how Margaret acted. And that was the last we saw of her.'

Barbara was still very shaken when she caught a bus to Waterloo. But by now she was certain that she'd imagined it. She must have become wound up about not being invited to the service.

Standing on the platform, she became so agitated that people round about kept their distance. As the train came into the station, she began to panic, muttering and talking aloud to herself. She suddenly recalled the moment when she'd been at the manor house and had felt someone pushing her down the stairs.

She tried to remember exactly what the detective had said. That a witness was sure Margaret had been pushed under the train. But that wasn't possible, as no one was standing close enough.

Barbara took deep breaths in an effort to

calm herself. Passengers were shooting wary glances in her direction.

She shouted, 'What are you looking at me for?'

As the train pulled out, she literally jumped when her mobile rang.

It was Mr Sullivan to say that if she required immediate funds he would be able to release a few thousand pounds.

'Thank you. That would be really helpful. In fact, I hope it's all right but I'm on my way to the manor house now.'

Mr Sullivan ummed and ahhed, but eventually said it would be fine.

Barbara paused. 'One more thing. I was so stunned at the time I don't really remember. As well as the house, exactly how much money will I inherit?'

'Miss Reynolds had accounts containing around three-quarters of a million pounds.'

'Three-quarters of a million,' she breathed.

By the time the train pulled into the local station, it was getting dark. Barbara was very buoyant, smiling at the ticket collector as she made her way out to the car park. The Land Rover was where she had left it, keys hidden away as before.

As she headed for the manor house she couldn't keep the smile off her face. Three-quarters of a million! She was brimming over with ideas for redecorating, making the sombre house lighter. She would get some nice sofas, make the place feel lived in. By the time she'd driven 'home', she was still buzzing.

She hesitated for a moment before she went into the oak-panelled hall. She would light a big fire. Make herself something to eat. In the morning she would take a tour of the entire house.

She tried the light switch by the open kitchen door. It clicked, but still nothing happened. She'd check out the generator tomorrow. By now she was familiar with the kitchen. She lit candles, then took some kindling and logs. She was pleased with herself. She was becoming very adept at fire-lighting.

Humming to herself, she went into the larder and chose a tin of chicken soup.

'Hello.'

Barbara froze.

'I've been waiting ages for you.'

The little girl was standing barefoot at the kitchen door. She had curly blonde hair and a sweet, angelic face. Dressed in jeans and a blue

T-shirt, she looked much happier than she had at the cemetery.

Barbara gasped, unable to believe what she was seeing.

'It's time for my piano lesson.'

Barbara shook her head. This was madness. The little girl moved closer.

'Stay away from me,' Barbara cried.

She knocked over the chair as she moved backwards. The child shimmered, at one moment clear and real, the next transparent.

'You promised on Mama's Bible to take care of me.'

Barbara pressed herself against the sink.

'Who are you?'

'I'm Emily. I'm seven years old. I'll be eight in two months' time.'

'No! No!' Barbara shouted.

'YES, YES, YES,' Emily shouted back gleefully. 'Come upstairs. It's time for my piano lesson.'

'No,' Barbara repeated.

She was terrified. Her heart felt as if it would burst out of her chest. She moved cautiously to the door.

Tink-tink-tink came the sound of the piano. Just as Barbara had heard when she stayed previously. She picked up a candlestick and, gritting her teeth, headed into the hall.

With her free hand on the banister, the other holding the candlestick on high, she moved up the stairs. She looked into the various rooms and headed up another floor. She moved towards where the sound of the piano was loudest. Scrawled writing on the wall read 'Emily's Room'.

The child carried on with her scales. Barbara edged further into the room. Emily stopped and swivelled round on the piano stool.

'Do you know "Chopsticks"? Aunt Margaret used to play with me.'

Barbara's mind was churning. This couldn't be happening.

'Margaret is dead,' she whispered.

'I know. She's gone to be with Mummy and Armande. She wanted that for such a long time. But she couldn't because there was no one to look after me.'

Emily swung round on the stool again, her legs dangling.

'I was conceived here. I was born here.'

'You're dead too,' Barbara said.

'Yes, but I'm alive for you, only you. And in return for taking care of me you inherit everything. Just like Aunt Margaret. I was her secret and now I'm yours.'

*

122

Barbara turned and hurried from the room. She made her way back to the kitchen, gulping for air. The panic attack was making her stumble and lurch around as she gasped for breath.

She leaned on the table, telling herself to calm down. She pinched her arm until it hurt and at last the dizzy feeling receded. Then she heard the footsteps running across the room above.

Needing the warmth, she sat close to the fire, going over in her mind every moment she had spent with Margaret. She recalled how she had placed her hand over the cross of the Bible. She had sworn she would never tell Margaret's secret. How could she explain what being Margaret's heir entailed? Who would believe her? They'd probably take her away, just like Margaret.

Barbara gave herself another hard pinch, to make sure she was awake.

Then she began to think . . .

Would it really be so bad? She was alone. She had always been alone.

Barbara sat a while in silence.

She didn't even take a candle to light her way back to the room. Walking slowly up the stairs, she pushed open the door and Emily turned towards her.

She was writing her ten times table on a blackboard with a piece of chalk.

'I can play "Chopsticks",' Barbara said softly.

She picked up a chair and placed it by the piano stool.

'I knew it would be you,' Emily said as she joined her.

'I will keep my promise, Emily. I will take care of you.'

Together they began to play the piano.

And Barbara realized that she had never felt so contented or at peace.

Acknowledgements

Special thanks and gratitude go to all my team at La Plante Productions: Liz Thorburn, Richard Dobbs-Grove, Cass Sutherland and Sara Johnson for all their committed and valuable support.

Many thanks also go to Duncan Heath and Sue Rodgers at Independent Talent Agency and Stephen Ross and Andrew Bennet-Smith at Ross, Bennet-Smith.

Many thanks for the constant encouragement from my literary agent Gill Coleridge and the team at Rogers, Coleridge & White.

The publication of this book would not have been possible without the hard work and support of Susan Opie, Lesley Levene and the team at Simon & Schuster: Ian Chapman, Suzanne Baboneau, Nigel Stoneman, Jessica Leeke and Rob Cox; I am very happy to be working with such a terrific and creative group of people.

Quick Reads 📖

Books in the Quick Reads series

Quick Reads 📖

Fall in love with reading

Quick Reads are brilliantly written short new books by bestselling authors and celebrities. Whether you're an avid reader who wants a quick fix or haven't picked up a book since school, sit back, relax and let Quick Reads inspire you.

We would like to thank all our funders:

We would also like to thank all our partners in the Quick Reads project for their help and support:

NIACE • unionlearn • National Book Tokens
The Reading Agency • National Literacy Trust
Welsh Books Council • Welsh Government
The Big Plus Scotland • DELNI • NALA

We want to get the country reading

Quick Reads, World Book Day and World Book Night are initiatives designed to encourage everyone in the UK and Ireland – whatever your age – to read more and discover the joy of books.

Quick Reads launches on **14 February 2012**
Find out how you can get involved at www.**quickreads**.org.uk

World Book Day is on **1 March 2012**
Find out how you can get involved at www.**worldbookday**.com

World Book Night is on **23 April 2012**
Find out how you can get involved at www.**worldbooknight**.org

Quick Reads 📖

Fall in love with reading

Doctor Who
Magic of the Angels

Jacqueline Rayner

BBC Books

*'No one from this time
will ever see that girl again ...'*

On a sight-seeing tour of London the Doctor wonders why so many young girls are going missing. When he sees Sammy Star's amazing magic act, he thinks he knows the answer. The Doctor and his friends team up with residents of an old people's home to discover the truth. And together they find themselves face to face with a deadly Weeping Angel.

Whatever you do – don't blink!

A thrilling all-new adventure featuring the Doctor, Amy and Rory, as played by Matt Smith, Karen Gillan and Arthur Darvill in the hit series from BBC Television.

Quick Reads 📖

Fall in love with reading

Full House

Maeve Binchy

Orion

Sometimes the people you love most
are the hardest to live with.

Dee loves her three children very much, but now they
are all grown up, isn't it time they left home?

But they are very happy at home. It doesn't cost them
anything and surely their parents like having a full
house? Then there is a crisis, and Dee decides things
have to change for the whole family . . . whether they
like it or not.

Quick Reads 📖

Fall in love with reading

Beyond the Bounty

Tony Parsons

Harper

Mutiny and murder in paradise …

The Mutiny on the Bounty is the most famous uprising in naval history. Led by Fletcher Christian, a desperate crew cast sadistic Captain Bligh adrift. They swap cruelty and the lash for easy living in the island heaven of Tahiti. However, paradise turns out to have a darker side …

Mr Christian dies in terrible agony. The Bounty burns. Cursed by murder and treachery, the rebels' dreams turn to nightmares, and all hope of seeing England again is lost forever …

Quick Reads 📖

Fall in love with reading

The Cleverness of Ladies

Alexander McCall Smith

Abacus

There are times when ladies must use
all their wisdom to tackle life's mysteries.

Mma Ramotswe, owner of the No.1 Ladies' Detective
Agency, keeps her wits about her as she looks into
why the country's star goalkeeper isn't saving goals.
Georgina turns her rudeness into a virtue when she
opens a successful hotel. Fabrizia shows her bravery
when her husband betrays her. And gentle La proves
that music really can make a difference.

With his trademark gift for storytelling, international
bestselling author Alexander McCall Smith brings us
five tales of love, heartbreak, hope and the cleverness
of ladies.

Quick Reads 📖

Fall in love with reading

Quantum of Tweed:
The Man with the Nissan Micra

Conn Iggulden

Harper

Albert Rossi has many talents. He can spot cheap polyester at a hundred paces. He knows the value of a good pair of brogues. He is in fact the person you would have on speed-dial for any tailoring crisis. These skills are essential to a Gentleman's Outfitter from Eastcote. They are less useful for an international assassin.

When Albert accidentally runs over a pedestrian, he is launched into the murky world of murder-for-hire. Instead of a knock on the door from the police, he receives a mysterious phone call.

His life is about to get a whole lot more interesting . . .

Other resources

Enjoy this book? Find out about all the others from
www.quickreads.org.uk

Free courses are available for anyone who wants to develop
their skills. You can attend the courses in your local area.
If you'd like to find out more, phone 0800 66 0800.

 Don't get by get on 0800 66 0800

For more information on developing your skills in Scotland
visit www.**thebigplus**.com

Join the Reading Agency's Six Book Challenge at
www.**sixbookchallenge**.org.uk

THE
READING
AGENCY

Publishers Barrington Stoke and New Island
also provide books for new readers.
www.**barringtonstoke**.co.uk • www.**newisland**.ie

The BBC runs an adult basic skills campaign.
See www.**bbc**.co.uk/**skillswise**

Skillswise